"He's going to win if we don't get some help!"

Holly tried to keep her voice calm. "I know this so deeply in my soul, Manda. I have to save him. My power merged with his can defeat his father."

"You don't know that! You can't know that!" Amanda shouted. Heads turned in their direction. "You're just figuring all this stuff out as we go along!"

"Shh, Manda," Tommy cautioned. "Michael might have spies around."

"We're not the ones he's after," Silvana said pointedly, her arm still around the bereft Kialish.

Holly felt a rush of shame. *I will kill them, one by one. I carry the curse. Will I take it to Jer? Will I kill him too?*

I have to find him. I know it. And I know it's not magic leading me to him. . . .

Wicked titles
by Nancy Holder and Debbie Viguie

Witch

Curse

Legacy
(coming soon)

Available from Simon Pulse

WICKED
CURSE

NANCY HOLDER *and* **DEBBIE VIGUIÉ**

SIMON PULSE
New York London Toronto Sydney Singapore

First Simon Pulse edition January 2003

Copyright © 2003 by Nancy Holder

SIMON PULSE
An imprint of Simon & Schuster
Children's Publishing Division
1230 Avenue of the Americas
New York, NY 10020

Design by Ann Sullivan
The text of this book was set in Aldine 401 BT.

Printed in the United States of America

10 9 8 7 6 5 4 3 2 1

Library of Congress Control Number 2002110488

ISBN 0-7434-2697-5

To my daughter, Belle, who is magical.

—Nancy Holder

To my husband, Scott, and the magic of true love.

—Debbie Viguié

ACKNOWLEDGMENTS

Thanks to my wonderful coauthor, Debbie, and her husband, Scott, for being friends I can count on. Thanks to our Simon & Schuster family, Lisa Clancy, Micol Ostow, and Lisa Gribbin. To my agent and his assistant, Howard Morhaim and Neeraja Viswanathan, my gratitude always.

—N. H.

Thanks to my coauthor and mentor, Nancy, for being such an inspiring writer and a dear friend. Thank you also to all the people without whom this would not be possible, most especially Termineditor Lisa. Thank you to all those who have offered me encouragement and shared the joy and pain of creativity: Chris Harrington, Marissa Smeyne, Teresa Snook, Amanda Goodsell, and Lorin Heller. Thank you also to George and Greta Viguié, the parents of my beloved husband. Without you he would not be the man he is.

—D. V.

CAST OF CHARACTERS

Forces of Light

Cathers/Anderson Coven

Ladies of the Lily—Cahors descendants

Holly Cathers—head of the coven, cousin to Amanda and Nicole

Amanda Anderson—the "boring" twin, daughter of Marie-Claire and Richard

Nicole Anderson—the "vibrant" twin, daughter of Marie-Claire and Richard

Others

Silvana Beaufrere—Amanda's childhood friend

Tante Cecile—a voodoo practitioner and Silvana's aunt

Tommy Nagai—Amanda's best friend

Rebel Coven

Jeraud Deveraux—warlock burned in the Black Fire, son of Michael

Kari Hardwicke—graduate student and Jeraud's former girlfriend

Kialish Carter—Jeraud's best friend

Eddie Hinook—Kialish's lover

Spanish Coven

José Luís—leader of the Spanish Coven
Philippe—José Luís's lieutenant
Armand—studied for the priesthood before he learned magic
Alonzo—the oldest member of the coven, their "father figure"
Pablo—José Luís's younger brother

Mother Coven

Sasha—mother of Jeraud and Eli
Anne-Louise Montrachet—raised in the Mother Coven, its representative

Forces of Darkness

Supreme Coven

Michael Deveraux—evil warlock, father of Jeraud and Eli
Eli Deveraux—Jeraud's brother, who is following in their father's footsteps
Sir William Moore—leader of the Supreme Coven
James Moore—Sir William's son, who is plotting to overthrow him

Ancestors

Isabeau Cahors—in love with and married to her sworn enemy, Jean, she betrayed both their families; her spirit is cursed to wander the world until she kills him

Jean Deveraux—married to Isabeau, he both loves her and hates her

Catherine Cahors—Isabeau's mother, the most powerful Cahors witch until Holly

Laurent Deveraux—Jean's father, the last warlock to possess the secret of the Black Fire

Others

Richard Anderson—father of Nicole and Amanda, who is unaware of their witchly heritage

Barbara Davis-Chin—the mother of Holly's friend who drowned, she is in a coma in San Francisco, a victim of Michael Deveraux

Dan Carter—Native American shaman

Part One
Waxing

☾

"When the moon in the sky begins to swell, all the world grows with her,
planning, scheming, waiting. It is at this time that the womb grows ripe
and all dark purposes are set in motion."

—Marcus the Great, 410

ONE

SINGING MOON

☾

We shout our defiance to the skies
To the sun shining in our eyes
The House of Deveraux has power
And it grows with every passing hour

Attend, anon, each Cahors Witch
For words alone can make us rich
The Crone bids us listen each hour
For words bring knowledge and knowledge power

Holly and Amanda: Seattle, the first moon after Lammas

In Autumn of the Coventry year, one reaps exactly what one sows, multiplied sevenfold. It is as true of the souls of the dead as it is of sheaves of grain and clusters of grapes.

A full year had passed since Holly Cathers's parents had drowned, and her best friend, Tina Davis-Chin, with them, whitewater rafting on the Colorado River. Death had invaded the Anderson home in

3

Seattle, taking Marie-Claire, the sister of Holly's father. Marie-Claire Cathers-Anderson lay rotting in one of the two plots she and her husband, Richard, had purchased together once upon a romantic dream of eternity. The reality of her adultery made it very hard for Uncle Richard to hope for another, better place where she waited for him—a fact that he told Holly often, now that he had taken to drinking late at night.

Tina's mother, Barbara Davis-Chin, lay sick in Marin County General back in San Francisco. She had once been an ER doc there with Holly's mom. Now that Holly had learned of the witchery world and taken her place at the head of her own coven, she knew Barbara's condition had been no accident.

Barbara's illness was Michael's first attack on us because he wanted me here in Seattle. I had planned to live with Barbara, but he needed me here . . . because he wanted to kill me.

Bolts of lightning sizzled overhead amid cascades of icy cold rain. Supercharged volts fanned out like search parties as their many-armed, air-splitting zig-zags slammed in to the earth. Holly felt very vulnerable in the family station wagon, a slow-moving duck wading through the puddles. Three blocks from Kari Hardwicke's place, she got out of the station wagon and ran the rest of the way.

Heavily warded, Holly wore a cloak of invisibility

4

Singing Moon

that Tante Cecile, a voodoo practitioner, and Dan Carter, a northwest Native American shaman, had worked together to create. She had taken to wearing it whenever she had to go out. The cloak was by no means perfect, often losing its power to conceal her, but Holly had worn it faithfully ever since they had gifted her with it less than a week after the battle of the Black Fire last Beltane.

The coven was waiting for her at Kari's grad student apartment, which was located in a funky reconverted Queen Anne mansion near the University of Washington at Seattle. Kari was the one who had demanded the coven convene for a Circle. Last night at three A.M.—the Dark Hour of the Soul—she had suddenly awakened from a terrible nightmare that she could not remember. Drawn to the window, she had watched in horror as monsters dove past her turret room—huge, jet-black creatures that she was almost certain were oversized falcons.

Falcons were the totem of the Deveraux family.

If Michael Deveraux had returned to Seattle, and if on top of that, he had found a way to rescue his evil son, Eli, the Cathers/Anderson Coven was in deep and possibly fatal trouble. Michael Deveraux longed to conclude the blood feud begun by the Cathers and Deveraux ancestors so many centuries ago. That

5

vendetta demanded no less than the death of every Cathers witch alive—namely Holly and her cousins, Amanda and Nicole.

As leader of the Cathers/Anderson Coven, it fell to Holly to protect them all and to save herself.

She had very little in the way of weaponry. She had known she was a witch for less than a year, while the Deveraux had never forgotten that their ancient lineage ranked them among the most hated and feared warlocks of all time. While her last name was Cathers, her ancestors had been of the noble witch house of Cahors, of medieval France. Over time their identity had been lost along with their real name. Holly believed that her father had known about the witch blood that ran in his veins, but she wasn't certain of that. She did know he had broken with the Seattle branch of the family, and it was only upon his death that Holly had learned he'd had a sister, and that she, Holly, had cousins.

Holly wondered what he would think if he knew she had reluctantly embraced her witch blood, and that she now led a full coven. Never mind that that coven was a ragtag mélange of traditions and powers, consisting of Amanda; Amanda's friend Tommy Nagai; Cecile Beaufrere, voodoo practitioner, and her daughter, Silvana; and the remnants of Jer's Rebel

Singing Moon

Coven—Eddie Hinook and his lover, Kialish Carter, and Jer's former lover, Kari Hardwicke. Kialish's father was the shaman who had helped with her cloak, but he had not formally joined the Circle.

The Cathers/Anderson Coven was like a tiny paper boat in an ocean, when compared to the forces of evil massed against it.

Lightning arced directly overhead, interrupting her worrying. It seemed these days she was always worried.

Along the street, faces glanced anxiously through rain-blurred windows as Holly ran past them. The inhabitants no doubt enjoyed a measure of comfort in the knowledge that lightning rods protected their houses. But Holly knew that if Michael Deveraux sent the lightning, no conventional protection would save a building from being burned to the ground.

"Goddess, breathe blessings on me," she murmured as she kept to the shadows and moved her fingers firmly shrouded in the cloak. "Protect my Circle. Protect me."

It had become her mantra . . . and sometimes, the only thing that kept her from panicking completely.

Every night, I go to sleep wondering if Michael Deveraux has returned to Seattle . . .

. . . and if I'll wake up the next morning.

7

★ ★ ★

In her anxiety over Holly's arrival, Amanda Anderson placed her face and hands against the cold window pane in the turret room of Kari Hardwicke's apartment. The scar crossing her right palm would give her away as a Cathers witch to any knowing set of eyes, be they bird or warlock; remembering that, she plucked her hands quickly from the glass and cradled them both against her chest.

Behind her, Tante—"Aunt," in French—Cecile Beaufrere and her daughter, Silvana, bustled around the apartment checking on the wards they and Dan Carter had helped Holly and Amanda install. The two had closed up their New Orleans house and moved back to Seattle to help Holly's coven fight the Deveraux. For their own personal protection, mother and daughter had woven amulets of silver and glass beads into the cornrows of their soft black hair, and they looked like Nubian warriors preparing for a great hunt.

"It would be better if Nicole were here," Silvana murmured. "The three Cathers witches united make stronger magic than just Holly and Amanda." Proof of that lay in the fact that each of the three bore a segment of the Cahors symbol, the lily, burned into her palm. Placed together, the cousins were stronger magically than they were separately.

But the three were only two in the current incarnation of the Circle. They had been reduced to two immediately after the Battle of the Black Fire. The reality of what they were doing had hit Amanda's sister, Nicole, too hard. She had run away, leaving Seattle behind, and the two remaining Cathers witches had no idea where she was.

While it was difficult for Amanda to blame her sister, it left everyone else weak and vulnerable to any potential attacks by the Deveraux. Holly had convinced the coven to spend the summer training, growing in the Art, and trying to work with Jer's followers. And all during that summer, they saw no trace of Michael Deveraux, head of the Deveraux Coven and Jer's father, whom Jer himself had repudiated. Nor had they seen Michael's older son, Eli, who had been carried off, burning with Black Fire, by an enormous magical falcon.

No one had seen a Deveraux since.

The screech of a bird echoed through the thunder. Holly glanced up, squinting through the rain. A flock of black birds soared and cartwheeled, tempest-tossed, their eyes flashing, their blue-black wings beating back the storm.

They were falcons.

Holly hurried on, reaching the apartment without alerting the birds—or so it appeared, and so she prayed—and Amanda opened the door before Holly could knock. Like Holly, Amanda had matured, her face thinner, her mousy hair streaked through with summer highlights. She was no longer the "boring" twin to Nicole's vibrant drama. She was steady and wise—in magical terms, a priestess. Holly was grateful to her core for Amanda's presence.

"Were you . . . did you get here okay?" Amanda asked, taking in Holly's sopping wet appearance.

"The car was too much of a target," Holly said. "I came on foot."

"Don't you own a broom yet?" That was Kari, who was terrified. Holly forgave her her snide comment, but she was tired of all the snipes Kari had shot her way over the past months.

She hates me, Holly thought. *She blames me for Jer's death.*

She's right. I killed him.

Holly cleared her throat as the others assembled, all facing her. They looked at her expectantly, as if she would know what to do now. The truth was, she had no idea.

"We need to form a circle. Who will be our Long Arm of the Law tonight?" she asked, gazing at the three men in their midst. As was common in many Wiccan traditions, in Holly's coven the women performed the magic while the men kept the circle safe from harm. She who conducted the rite was the coven's designated High Priestess. Her male counterpart was called the Long Arm of the Law. In the Cathers/Anderson Coven, he cut all harm with a very splendid old sword, which Tante Cecile had located in an antique shop and the coven had infused with magic.

"I'll serve," Tommy said, inclining his head.

"Then kneel," Holly instructed him, "and receive my blessing."

He got down on his knees. Amanda came forward with a beautifully carved bone dipper of oil in which floated Holly's favorite magical herb, rosemary. The herb was associated with remembrance; it boggled Holly that her family had carried Cahors witch blood in their veins for centuries, and yet the memory had been lost.

Holly moved her hands over the oil, silently invoking the Goddess, while Silvana presented the sword to the circle and placed it between Tommy's clasped hands. It was made of bronze, and extremely heavy. Runes and sigils had been carved into the hilt and etched in acid on the blade, but no one in the coven—not even Kari, who, as a graduate student, was steeped in the knowledge of various magic traditions and folkways—had been able to translate or decipher any of them.

Tommy breathed deeply, becoming one with the sword and with Holly's own rhythmic breaths. The rest took their places around Holly and Tommy in the circle, forming a living, single magical being.

We're one, Holly thought. *We have a power the Deveraux do not. Through love, we are trying to break down our barriers and work fully together. Their system is based on power, wresting it away from others and holding on to it at all costs. And I have to believe that love is stronger than that.*

"I bless your brow, for wisdom's sake," she said, making a pentagram with oil on his forehead.

"I bless your eyes, for good vision and sharp sight." She dotted each closed eyelid with more oil.

"I bless your sense of smell, for detection of hellish sulfur." She ran a line of oil down his nose.

She blessed his mouth, that he might call out a warning in case of attack. She blessed his heart, for courage, and his arms, for the strength to wield his sword well against trespassers.

Then she deliberately placed her thumb on the sharp edge of the sword, wincing as she cut herself. Drops of blood ran down the blade, feeding it.

Love might be the coin of the realm, but blood still fed the circle. The Cahors had not been a gentle house; in their day they had been just as ruthless as the Deveraux. What Holly hoped for was evolution, a chance to reinvent her family's path. Since so much had been lost in the intervening centuries, she was trying to find the balance between new magical forms and the traditions her coven must observe in order for the magic to work. It was slow going, a process of trial and error . . . but if Michael was back to threaten them, she would have to do whatever it took to keep her people safe, no matter how "unevolved" it was.

But this was not the time for such ruminations; she quickly finished Tommy's anointing.

"I bless you from crown to heel, Tommy. Rise, my Long Arm of the Law, and embrace your priestess."

Tommy stood tall as Holly handed the dipper back to Amanda. Then she put her arms around him, careful not to touch the sword with her body, and kissed him gently on the lips.

She took a step backward, and Tommy said, "I will sever any snares our enemies have set."

"Blessed be," the circle murmured.

Amanda and Kari let go of each other's hands, allowing Tommy to pass.

"I will smite our enemies' imps and familiars, be they invisible or disguised," he continued.

"Blessed be," the circle said again.

With great effort, he raised the sword toward the ceiling.

"And I—"

A terrible scream shattered the moment. Something flashed, glowing green. Wind whipped through the room, frigid and solid like ice. The stench of sulfur invaded the space.

Tommy staggered backward. "Look!" Kari screamed, pointing.

Grunting, Tommy jabbed the sword tip toward the ceiling. The glow was pierced; a phosphorescent, semiliquid stream of green tumbled around the sword tip and dripped onto the floor. Kari jumped away from it, and the rest of the circle struggled to keep their hands clasped.

The glow vibrated, then faded.

"Oh, my God," Kari gasped.

Skewered on the tip of the sword was the likeness of a falcon jerking in its death throes. It was not a real bird, but a magical representation; the green glow thickened and became blood, steaming and fresh. Tommy's hands were coated with it, and it was dripping onto the floor.

As Holly stared in dread fascination, the bird's mouth dropped open. A disembodied voice echoed throughout the room:

"You Cahors whores, you'll be dead by midsummer."

With one last shudder, the bird stopped moving. Its eyes stared dully out at the circle.

There was a silence.

Then Amanda said, "He's back. Michael Deveraux is back."

Holly closed her eyes; dread and stark fear washed over her.

Here we go, she thought. *The battle lines have just been drawn. How can we possibly fight him?*

More to the point . . . how can we hope to beat him?

Nicole: Cologne, Germany, September

Nicole threw a terrified glance over her shoulder as she raced down the corridors of the train station. A train rumbled away; her footsteps echoed like staccato points to the bass line of its leave-taking. The pink and gold streaks of dawn chased the shadows, and she was terribly grateful; the night had held sway far too long, and she was exhausted.

I should have stayed in Seattle, she thought. *I thought I'd be safer if I ran away . . . but there's that old saying about dividing and conquering . . . except that I don't know what it is. . . .*

Ever since she'd been in London three months ago, something had been following her. It was not a person, not in the traditional sense; it was something that could glide along the walls of buildings and perch on gabled rooftops—something that could trail after her with a rush of wings and a lone cry. She had not been able to see it; but in her mind, it was a falcon, and it was Michael Deveraux's eyes and ears, harrying her like the little mouse she was.

She wasn't certain that it had ever actually located her. Perhaps it was blindly lurking, waiting for her to use magic to reveal herself. That idea gave her hope that she might survive long enough to figure out what to do. *I'm terrified to contact Holly and Amanda. . . . What if that reveals my presence to whatever this thing is? Like answering "Polo" when the blindfolded guy who's saying "Marco" is six inches away from you?*

She was on her way to holy ground; she had covered much of Europe from London to France to Germany by leapfrogging from church to graveyard to chapel to cathedral. She didn't know if her gut instinct to seek safe harbor in mosques, synagogues, and Christian churches was correct. All she knew was that she felt better within walls built by people who adhered to some sort of faith tradition . . . as if their faith protected her from evil.

She listened to that instinct and to the urge to keep moving. The shadow was following her, and she had the feeling that if she kept moving, it might never land on her—might not carry her off, the way that huge falcon had carried off Eli.

Did he die?

What about Holly and Amanda? I abandoned them. I'm so ashamed. I was so scared. . . .

She had ridden a train all night. Her destination this dawn was the famous Dom of Cologne, an ancient medieval cathedral said to house relics of the Three Kings. She had read about it in a guidebook; she had bought and memorized more guidebooks about religious buildings in Europe than could be carried in a fully stocked travel store. She had taken an enormous number of trains. She had spent tons of money.

Problem is, I'm almost out of money. . . . What am I going to do when I can't run anymore?

Up the steps, she stopped. A hundred feet away, rising at the edge of a square, the tall Gothic structure loomed like a monolith. Its spire stretched toward the heavens; the rosettes and statues that cluttered the entry were dark gray, welcoming.

Gray magic is what the Cathers are all about, she thought. *Our ancestors, the Cahors, were not very good people. They were just . . . less evil than the Deveraux.*

We aren't necessarily the good guys.

17

Still, heaven seems happy to shelter us.

Taking a deep breath, Nicole raced across the square and pushed open the doors of the church.

It was cool inside; a row of men in brown robes tied with black sashes stood with their backs to her and sang in Latin. A priest in a collar raised his eyes inquiringly; she knew he saw a young woman in jeans and a peasant top, carrying a backpack. Her dark hair was coiled on top of her head and she wore no makeup. She was sunburned and there were circles under her eyes.

In three months Nicole had had an unbroken night of sleep exactly twice.

I'm so tired and scared.

Scowling at her, the priest waved his finger in her face. *"Hier darf man nicht schlafen, verstehen Sie?"* he asked her sternly. *Do you understand that you may not sleep in here?*

"Ja," she said breathlessly. Her eyes welled with tears, and the man immediately softened.

He walked a few steps backward, gesturing to the pews. There were no other people there except for the row of monks singing an early-morning Mass.

Nicole inclined her head and said, *"Danke schön."* "Thank you" was one of the "Useful Words and Phrases" she had memorized from one of her guidebooks.

She slid into the nearest pew and sat back, staring up at the celestial heights of the arched ceiling high above her. As she let the atmosphere of the church permeate her being, she could visualize the sun piercing the darkness above the spire.

And then, in her mind's eye, a dark shadow flitted between her and the sun.

She gasped aloud. The traveling shadow was the silhouette of a bird. And she sat inside this deceptive trap like a doomed, helpless mouse.

Then the church bells ran pealing out the message, *All is well, all is well.*

And that was a damn lie.

Jer: The Island of Avalon, October

The lie was that this was being alive.

Each instant that he lived was an eternity of torment. Each breath he took was a bellows in his chest, stoking the Black Fire flames as they roasted his heart and his lungs.

If he had been capable of coherent thought, Jer Deveraux would have begged the God to let him die. And beneath that supplication would have fluttered the terrible fear that he was dead already . . . and in Hell.

Echoing through his throbbing skull, words he

could not comprehend told the tale of the rest of his unbearable existence: "If you have not killed Holly Cathers by midsummer, Michael, I will kill your son and feed his soul to my servants."

And Michael Deveraux had answered, "I am yours to command in this and all things."

From her perch in the shimmering blue mist that was the magic of the Cahors, the lady hawk, Pandion, ruffled her feathers and cocked her head. She heard a plaintive cry, as that from a mate, and prepared to take flight in search of it.

And from the green-glowing ether that was his rookery, Fantasme, the falcon familiar of the Deveraux, sharpened his talons on the skull of a long-dead foe.

Holly and Amanda: Seattle, October

We are all still alive. It's been almost a month since the apparition of the falcon in our Circle, and we have managed to keep Michael Deveraux at bay.

Holly stared out at the ocean, allowing its vastness to sweep over her, engulf her until she felt small once more. She drew strength from her solitary walks along the shore; sometimes she wondered if Isabeau's ghost walked with her, supporting her as she struggled to keep the coven together and to keep them safe from

Michael Deveraux. There was power in the heartbeat of the waves, the ebb and flow of the great waters. The ocean was in its turn mother, lover, and enemy. The gentle, rhythmic lap of the waves was like the soothing beating of a mother's heart as she cradled her baby.

Holly closed her eyes and let herself listen to the sound. She breathed in the fresh salty air, and for a moment she might have been anywhere—in San Francisco, her old home even, instead of her new one in Seattle.

Tears squeezed out from beneath her closed eyelids and rolled slowly down her cheeks. It had not been a good day. Any day you had to start with a phone call to your lawyer was not a good day.

Holly was only nineteen, yet dealing with her parents' attorney had become a part of her life. Between talking to him and the financial planner who helped oversee her inheritance, she thought she might scream. There were always questions to answer and more papers to sign. They wanted to discuss her finances and her options for the future.

What if I have no future? What if I die tomorrow? she thought, a wave of bitterness choking her. *I'm fighting for my life, for the lives of my family and friends, and nobody gets it. I don't have time to worry about what I'm going to do five years from now. I probably won't even be here.*

Still, she knew that she should be grateful. If it weren't for her parents' careful planning, she wouldn't have time to practice spells and learn all the practical things that could help extend her life. She would be too busy trying to work to keep herself fed. It was especially important now that Uncle Richard had given up all pretext of going to work. Good thing Aunt Marie-Claire had money, or Amanda would be in serious trouble.

In a way she envied Kari. The older girl still at least got to pretend that she had a life, something other than magic and spells. She was still going to grad school. Tommy and Amanda were trying to go to college as well. Holly knew that Amanda in particular, though, was struggling. Holly figured college was just one of those dreams she herself had to give up the day that she learned she was a witch. *And that other people want to kill me.*

She sighed heavily. The day had only gone from bad to worse when she had called the hospital to check on Barbara. Most weeks the news was the same: no change in status. This week, though, she could sense something, an uneasiness in the doctor's voice that hadn't been there seven days before. Something was wrong; she could feel it. She was sure that Barbara was somehow doing worse. *And the doctors won't admit it.*

She felt herself begin to tremble. Barbara was her last tie to her own home, her parents, her childhood. Half a dozen times she had wanted to go to see her, to reassure herself that Barbara was truly still alive. But there were always more spells to learn, more protection rituals to perform. And there was the deep, dark fear in the back of her mind that if she got close to her, Barbara would die. *Everything I love withers.*

So she had come to the ocean to lose herself in its vastness, to seek its solace. The sea had comforted her before, and she prayed that it would again.

The waves reached up gently and tickled her toes, their caress soft and persuasive. The water called to her to come, explore, be one with it and its power. A tempting offer from a tempestuous lover. But Holly knew that the ocean could whisper words of soft promise one moment and then turn on you the next. It could change in seconds and kill so easily.

Never turn your back on it. Her father had told her that when she was five. She had been splashing in the waves for an hour when her mother called her to go put on more sunscreen. She had turned and tried to run out of the water. A huge wave had come out of nowhere and knocked her down. The undertow had sucked at her body, threatening to pull her out farther with it. She remembered trying to struggle, but the current had been too strong for her and she couldn't stand up or get her head out of the water.

Daddy had swooped in and picked her up, carrying her carefully from the water and stepping backward the entire time. He had deposited her, frightened and crying, into her mother's protective arms. She would never forget the look in his eyes as he bent down.

Never turn your back on the ocean, Holly. It may be beautiful, but it is also very dangerous.

She shivered now as an icy wind whipped around her and a wave slapped at her ankles. She took an involuntary step backward. Another wave slapped at her and she hopped back another step. The sound of the ocean was changing; instead of a gentle lapping sound, a dull roar jangled in her ears.

Startled, she had no time to react before a fresh wave crashed into her, soaking her in an instant in icy water waist-high and grasping at her with invisible hands.

The undertow pulled at her and she nearly lost her footing as she stumbled backward, shock quickly changing to fear. *You are not five!* her mind shouted at her as she fought to make it up onto the sand when another wave crashed around her chest. It knocked her off her feet and swept her several yards out.

I'll be swept out to sea! Oh, my God, is this happening?

Her long skirt wound around her legs, binding them like a mermaid's tail. Her arms were dead weights inside her heavy jacket. She could barely move, much less swim.

The fresh burst of panic focused her attention. *I have to get out of these clothes.*

"Goddess, grant me strength in battle and from death," she murmured in a Spell of Protection. Whether it worked or she was buoyed by the thought that she was never truly alone, she managed to snake first one arm and then the other out of her heavy jacket. It bobbed in the waves like a bloated jellyfish.

She worked on her skirt next, but her hands fumbled at the drawstring. She couldn't manage it; still terribly bogged down, she turned and tried to start swimming back to shore using only her arms. Within seconds, she was exhausted. Then a wave crashed over her and she coughed violently as her lungs dispelled the water she had just sucked in.

No sooner had she managed that, though, than another wave crested over her head. And another. Her brain began to numb and it locked on to the horrible images of the rafting trip that had claimed the lives of her parents and best friend. *It's been a year and now the water has come for me,* she thought fuzzily.

I'm not the same helpless girl I was then, though. I'm a

witch, and a powerful one. I should be able to do something to save myself.

She turned to look out to sea, her legs wearily treading water. What was it bodysurfers did? They rode the waves.

I can do that, too.

A huge wave began rolling in; Holly took a quick breath. "I can do this!" she cried as the wave reached her.

Her body was tossed up into the air, and then she was on top of the water, slightly in front of the crest of the wave.

She flew with dizzying speed toward the shore. Almost upon the beach, the wave broke behind her and threw her up onto the sand. Her mouth and eyes filled with the stinging granules as she clawed her way wildly up away from the water.

At last the strength in her limbs gave out and she collapsed, barely managing to roll onto her back as she coughed weakly. Her eyes stung and her face was raw, as though sand had been forcefully shoved into every pore and crevice. Her eyes began to tear fiercely and she let herself cry—to flush out her eyes, and to flush out her terror.

I nearly died. As I should have a year ago.

Don't be ridiculous. I was not "supposed" to die. I was meant to live. I have a coven to run, followers to protect.

At last the tears stopped flowing; she blinked rapidly trying to clear her vision. Slowly the sky shifted into focus . . . and it was low and dark and menacing.

The air was heavy; it almost seemed to crackle. She glanced quickly around. Nothing seemed familiar. Had the wave washed her up farther down the beach?

Electricity crackled down her spine as she slowly straightened. There was magic here and it felt very, very old. Feeling strangely compelled, she turned around so that her back was to the ocean.

Oh, my . . .

TWO

FALLING LEAF MOON

We grow stronger with each death
Reborn with each foe's last breath
With each sacrifice we renew
Our oaths to the Lord, loyalty true

We spin the wheel of the year
And know there is no cause to fear
For truth it is, that what has died
Strengthens us and dwells inside

The castle was ancient but beautiful. It called to her in a high tenor chant like a medieval troubadour telling the stories of King Arthur and his court. She felt as though she were floating as she moved toward it, her footsteps silent. The vast heap of stones was alive; she could feel it.

"Something wonderful happened here," she whispered.

A shadow crossed her mind. "And also something horrible."

Somehow she had covered the ground between her and the great walls without noticing. She reached out her hand to touch the weathered stone and her fingers tingled where they made contact. Power surged through the wall. It reached up her arm and wrapped itself around her, as though to bind her to itself for all eternity.

From within, something called to her, though she could not have told how or who. She placed her whole hand against the stone and leaned against it. Slowly, her flesh melted into the wall, merged with it, passed through it. As her hand went, the rest of her followed.

For a moment everything was dark and damp; fear rose again in her mind, and she thought, *I'm drowning in the ocean; it's a trick!*

The panicky moment passed, though, just as she passed through the wall. She turned to stare at the wall for a moment, to marvel in amazement.

Something still called her, compelled her to follow. . . .

She passed through wall after wall. The last wall proved a challenge, resisting her pushing at first, but finally giving way to her efforts. She found herself in a room luxuriant with light and warmth from a fire blazing in a great hearth. When at last she stepped completely through, she realized that she was not alone in the room.

Falling Leaf Moon

Seated before the fire was a man with his head on his fists. She walked up slowly behind him, without even a whisper of sound to give herself away. *Who is he? Why does he sit with shoulders slumped in despair?*

He must have felt something, for he looked up quickly, dropping his hands down toward his sides with a heavy clink.

She understood: Shackles bound the man's wrists and ankles. Holly reached out to touch the band about his left wrist but was painfully repulsed. The man was a captive, both physically and magically.

What could be his crime?

"Living," he answered.

She jumped backward, startled. She had not spoken out loud; how had he heard her?

"I can feel you, even though I can't see you." His voice was hoarse, yet hauntingly familiar. "It *is* you, isn't it, Holly?"

He turned his face directly toward her, and for one brief moment she thought he saw her. She shrank backward, but his eyes passed over her and continued on, sweeping the area around her.

And now she could see his face clearly, or rather, what was left of it.

"Jer!" she gasped.

"I'm not so sure of that anymore," he answered

31

grimly, fixing in on the location of the sound and staring unnervingly at her left earlobe.

He held up his left hand, and in the flickering light from the fire Holly could see that it was horribly scarred.

"A souvenir. A reminder of how close I came to death and how much I've lost by being alive."

She didn't understand his words, but she tucked them away in her mind. There would be time later to decipher his meaning.

"Where are we?" she asked.

He shrugged. "The island of Avalon."

She gasped. "Then this must be . . ."

"Yes. There is powerful magic in these walls. The Supreme Coven has owned this land ever since the death of the dark warlock Merlin. He worked his spells within these walls."

"Merlin? Supreme Coven? But where is it? Where is Avalon?" she asked, growing desperate. Something was pulling at her; she was slipping away.

Then he reached out to her, hands stretched and shaking with the effort from the weight and magic of them.

"Holly," he said hoarsely, "don't come. I couldn't help myself, couldn't stop myself from sending my soul out. You are my other half, and I am yours. But don't come. Exist without me, forever if you have to. Even though you won't be complete."

He gazed at her with longing, with love, with despair. "Don't look for me," he said.

"I—" Before she could promise him—*No, I won't promise; I will find you!*—she was ripped away. Back she sailed through all the walls, faster and faster, an undertow pulling at her, the pain accumulating, the hurt to her lungs profound—the hurt to her heart even more so.

She slammed against the last wall, and it groaned for a moment beneath her weight before giving way.

Pain surged through her right ankle.

Then she was back on the shore, in pitch darkness, running as fast as she could toward the water. Unseen hands hastened her along, and when she reached the ocean, they pushed her in.

The undertow caught her and dragged her so far out to sea that she could no longer see the shore.

Oh, my God, no. I was safe. Don't do this to me. Don't pull me out. I was safe!

Angry and frightened, she tried to fight the waves, to struggle back toward the unseen land.

A wave washed over her head and she closed her eyes tight against it. When at last she reopened them, it was once again daylight. The sun was yellow, tired, and wan, but it was shining.

There, not more than fifteen yards away, was the Seattle beach where she had been standing right before getting pulled into the water.

Holly gasped and swallowed sea water. She began coughing desperately. She was going through it all again, exactly as she had moments—*minutes? hours?* before. Remembering the huge wave, she turned and looked for it. There it was! She took a breath, offered up the same words, and felt the surge of power as the wave picked her up and carried her to the beach.

It took just as long to cry the sand out of her eyes, but when she opened them this time, Amanda was staring down at her.

Nicole: Spain, October

Cologne had frightened Nicole out of Germany.

Now in Spain, she moved like a hunted creature. Banners were up in the store windows to celebrate Halloween, presented as an American holiday; now it was late, the stores were closed, and no one walked the cobblestone streets. Silence hung thick like a blanket in this place whose look, whose feel, whose very smell was foreign to her. Nicole wrinkled up her nose. Coming to Madrid had seemed like a good idea at the time; there were hundreds of chapels, a cathedral, churches by the score.

But suddenly she wasn't so sure she should be there.

It feels very wrong.

A noise behind her caused her to twist. She forced herself to relax as the stumbling drunk waved at her before veering off on his way home, perhaps to an expected chastening from his long-suffering wife.

She folded her arms tight across her chest and forced herself to walk. The youth hostel she had checked in to was not that far, and at the moment she wanted nothing more than to be tucked into her little bed, safe and asleep.

I wish I were back home in Seattle. As it had a hundred times before, the thought came unbidden to her mind and she waved a hand in the air, as if she could push away the thoughts and feelings bombarding her: grief, relief, fear, homesickness.

She and her mom had started practicing magic because she had learned a few tricks from Eli. It had been fun, a secret game the two of them had played. Corn dollies and sympathetic magic.

The stakes have risen considerably, she thought wryly.

Nicole shivered. She had seen too much in the past year. Too much death, too much horror. *Too much magic.* The power that she had felt when she linked with Holly and Amanda had been terrifying. She couldn't deal with it. *And so here I am, in the middle of Spain trying to forget who and what I am.*

Another sound, a soft step perhaps, reached Nicole's ears. This time the hair on the back of her neck stood on end. Someone was behind her, she could feel it. She increased her speed, desperately fighting the urge to glance behind and see who or what was there.

Don't let it be a bird; don't let it be a bird; please, especially, don't let it be a falcon.

Suddenly she heard it, the crackle of electricity. She threw herself to the side just as a bolt of lightning ripped through the place where she had been standing. She landed hard on her side and twisted quickly to see where the attack had come from. Pain knifed through her. A cloaked figure stood ten feet away, laughing crazily.

"This is my home, witch. You have no business being here," a hissing female voice informed her.

"I'm not . . . not a witch," Nicole stammered.

"You lie! I can feel it. And since you have trespassed you shall be punished."

The figure raised its arms and began chanting in a strange tongue.

Nicole half-stumbled to her feet, every protection spell she had ever known fleeing her mind. She was helpless. She turned to run, opened her mouth to cry out, and fell against another hooded figure.

She screamed as she stared up to where the face should have been. All she could see was darkness. From the darkness a voice began to speak in a low, commanding tone. Nicole pushed herself away and took a half-step in the direction of the witch. What she saw brought her up short.

Four other cloaked figures had materialized as if from air. One of them extended an arm and the witch collapsed to the ground, clawing at her throat.

"Philippe, what have you done?" the figure behind her shouted in English.

"I only took her speech until such time as she is able to speak civilly to a stranger." That voice was very French.

Nicole whirled back to face the figure she had fallen against. Slowly, long, pale hands reached up to pull back the hood. A shock of dark curly hair framed a handsome face with piercing eyes. A wry smile twisted his lips as he looked down at Nicole.

"Welcome to Madrid, little *bruja*. I am José Luís, warlock and servant of the White Magic. And these," he added, gesturing to the others as they also removed their hoods, "are my friends."

★ ★ ★

On the beach, Holly stared up at Amanda.

"What happened?" she asked slowly.

"I was going to ask you that," Amanda retorted. "God, Hol, did you fall in?"

"I . . . I don't know." She grimaced at her wet clothes. "I . . . I dreamed or something." She looked back up at her cousin. "How did you find me?"

"I've been looking for you everywhere," Amanda said.

"What's wrong?" Holly demanded.

Amanda shook her head grimly. "I'll explain in the car. Let's go."

She reached down and, clasping Holly's hand, helped her to stand. Holly leaned gratefully on her cousin as they hurried toward the car.

"I'm soaking wet," Holly protested as Amanda opened the passenger door of Richard's car.

Amanda gave her a gentle shove. "Get in. We've got bigger things to worry about than upholstery."

Holly acquiesced and sat down, grimacing at the squishing sounds her clothes made as they encountered the seat. She didn't even have time to put on her seat belt before Amanda started the car, put it in gear, and floored it.

Holly scrambled to buckle herself in. As they flew around a corner, Holly smacked her head painfully against the window. She could feel more sea water dripping out of her ears as her head tilted.

"Ouch! Slow down, Amanda!"

"No time," Amanda muttered between clenched teeth.

Amanda cast a quick glance her way before putting the car into another sliding turn, tires screaming in outrage.

Another corner and Holly's stomach lurched even more. When the car straightened out, she looked at Amanda. The other girl's jaw was set and her face was pale—too pale. A faint trickle of blood crept down the side of her forehead and started tracing a path down her cheek.

Shocked, Holly saw a lump on the side of Amanda's head and noted that her hair was clumped and bloody around it.

"Michael's pumping up the volume," Amanda explained. "I was attacked at the house by some kind of invisible force. So I called Kari's house. No answer. Silvana and Tante Cecile's. Nothing. No Tommy, either. I worked my way down the list, and no one's picking up. So I figured: headquarters. Which for the time being is Kari's apartment. But I didn't want to go there without you."

Another corner forced Holly to turn her attention

back to the road, and she wished she knew a spell that could keep her from heaving.

Holly said weakly, "That sounds bad. Punch the turbo."

They arrived at Kari's apartment complex about a minute too late for Holly's stomach. She staggered from the car, collapsed onto her knees, and thought she might be sick—again. Amanda bounded from the driver's seat and headed for Kari's door at a dead run.

Amanda shouted from inside the apartment, and Holly pulled herself back up to her feet and stumbled toward the door. Inside, an overwhelming stench of gas caused her to fall to her knees and retch again.

In the corner Amanda was frantically working over four inert forms. She looked up and shouted, "Holly, turn the gas off!"

Unable to stand, Holly crawled to the kitchen, coughing and gagging the entire way. She made it to the oven and checked it. Everything was off.

"The pipes must have burst!" Holly forced herself to shout.

"Then come help me!" Amanda yelled.

Holly dragged herself out of the kitchen and over to Amanda. Her head was starting to spin and she felt herself losing focus. Suddenly Amanda clasped her palm and Holly felt the now-familiar surge of power that pulsated around them and through them. Her head cleared and she stared Amanda in the eyes.

Together they began to chant over their four friends.

Slowly Tommy stirred and looked up at them. "Something is binding us," he slurred.

Together Amanda and Holly passed their hands through the air over Tommy's body until they could feel something break free. He sat up abruptly and turned to help the other three.

Kialish, Eddie, and then Kari woke and were freed. At last the six of them stumbled to the door and made it outside just as the gas inside sparked.

They fell to the ground as a ball of fire washed over the top of them. In unison they began chanting. The skies opened up and rain poured down, dousing the flames. The thick waters quickly snuffed out the fire inside the apartment.

"Cool!" an onlooker cried appreciatively.

Holly turned to see one of the other grad students at the college standing and staring.

"Talk about your synchronicity. Fire, then rain."

"Amazing," Holly said weakly.

Then she got sick again.

Michael: Seattle

I almost had them this time, Michael thought as he paced in front of the altar in his Seattle home. *It went wrong somewhere.* He turned and raised his hands in angry fists. He would have his revenge. The witches would still pay.

Laurent, his ancestor, would know what to do. The phantom knew more than Michael wished . . . including the fact that, just as in 1666, the Deveraux Coven had recently been censured by the leader of the Supreme Coven, the most powerful ruling body on the warlock side of Coventry.

"Laurent! My lord and master, prithee, come to me," Michael petitioned, in perfect medieval French.

Nothing.

"Laurent," Michael called, respectfully. *"Je vous en prie.* A moment?"

"I think you'd rather talk to me," a voice behind him chortled.

Michael whirled around and found himself staring at a tiny creature. It was black and misshapen, its face broad and flat like a frog's, its nose more of a demonic snout, and fangs curled over the narrow lips. Its eyes were reptilian, green, and virtually spinning with madness.

"Where is my ancestor?" Michael asked carefully. He had no idea what this thing was doing here; for all he knew, it was here to kill him.

"I have a ssssecret," the creature informed him in a sing-song voice.

It's an imp, Michael thought. *I've heard of them; never seen one. . . . Laurent may have sent one instead of answering my call himself.*

"A ssssecret," the imp reiterated.

Michael stared at it. The thing rubbed its hands, one over the other, each finger ending in a slice of cartilage that was more than a fingernail, less than a bone. It was hunched and very, very ugly.

The imp wagged its brow above elongated, hate-filled eyes. "I know about the curse," it bragged.

"Curse? What curse?" Michael demanded in his most authoritative tone of voice.

The imp chittered like a squirrel. It bobbed and swayed as if it were completely mad.

"The curse against your sworn enemies."

A cautious smile tugged at Michael's lips. "Cahors?" he asked carefully. Then, in case his usage of the ancient name confused the creature, he added, "Cathers?"

"Yessss." The imp nodded, leaning forward as if to share something very, very interesting. "They don't like water much."

"And why is that?" Michael asked, enjoying for the moment a bit of fencing.

The imp pulled back its lips, exposing its teeth as it

grinned wildly at him. It said in a low, dramatic voice, "They tend to drown. That is the curse your ancestors laid on them. Drowning."

Michael was disappointed. The crazed, repulsive thing didn't know what it was talking about. If that was true, then Holly would have drowned in the ocean three days ago when he had tried to suck her in, or a year before, in the river with her parents.

"You're talking of dunking witches," he said dismissively. "If they float, they're guilty. If they drown, they're inno—"

The imp shook its head impatiently. "No, no, they *tend* to drown, true," the imp said. It pointed a single, scaly finger skyward. "But their loved ones *always* do. That is the curse laid upon the Cahors witches. By one of your own ancestors, may I hasten to add." It smiled again, as if it were about to fling itself at Michael and chew his face off his skull.

"Indeed," Michael said slowly.

"Indeed," the imp assured him.

A smile—*ah, the possibilities!*—spread across Michael Deveraux's face.

France, 13th century

"Your daughter, *madame,*" the emissary from the Deveraux announced with a flourish. Bowing over his leg, he gestured to the liveried servant who had accompanied him. The other man, a mere villein dressed up like a peacock in Deveraux red and green, smirked as he opened a small ebony box and tipped it over.

Ashes and small pieces of bone spilled onto the carpet that ran the length of the Great Hall of Castle Cahors. Like motes in the dying afternoon twilight, all that was left of Catherine's only child drifted down; sparkles of blue—the remnants of her witch blood's essence—caught the light like tiny sapphires, or the very tears of the Goddess herself.

Seated on her carved wooden throne, wearing a formal gown of mourning black, her hair pulled back and covered with a veil, Catherine, High Priestess of the Cahors Coven, remained stiff-lipped, but her heart caught in her throat. Though she knew that Isabeau had burned to death in the fire, the evidence still shook her. But she was a queen, and the daughter of kings and queens; she had lost kinsmen in the Crusades, in other battles, assassinations, and duels. Death was no stranger to her family, nor was the concept of sacrificing one of their own to further the ambitions of the family.

On the walls of her Great Hall, swords, shields, spears, lances, and battle axes hung crossed, in rows, and in circles. There was no room on the walls of the

Romanesque room for art, only the stark realities of her existence. Each moment, each day that the Cahors house continued could be counted a victory. Without her vigilance, the Deveraux would have surely found a way to grind the bones of all the Cahors to dust and ash, and to parade their triumph before stricken Coventry, now faced with the prospect of an unchecked and savage family of warlocks—the Deveraux.

Beyond her casement window, smoke still roiled from the ruins of Deveraux castle, the result of her carefully orchestrated scheme to burn the warlocks in their beds. Her daughter, Isabeau, had been instrumental in that, betraying Jean, heir of the Deveraux Coven, to whom she had been wed mere months before.

All would have been well if they had shared the secret of the Black Fire with us, she thought angrily as the last of Isabeau's ashes filtered to the carpet. *They forced my hand, and they know it.*

Retaliation is inevitable, and it will be brutal. Of that I have no doubt.

"What makes you think that you can mock my grief in this manner and then leave my castle alive?" she asked the Deveraux emissary.

"Honor," he said simply.

She regarded him. "Whose?"

"I carried a flag of truce," he reminded her, "when my horse cantered into your bailey. Your husband, Duc Robert, gave me safe passage so that I might bring your loved one home to you."

"I see." Her tone was almost conversational as she rose from her throne, descended the three steps from the dais, and crossed to the vast array of weaponry at her disposal. "And as a Deveraux, you assumed that his word carried more weight than mine, though I am the High Priestess of our coven?"

For the first time, the man looked uncertain.

"He guaranteed my safety," he stated flatly.

Without another word, she plucked a battle-axe off the wall, whirled around, took quick aim, and flung it directly at his head.

It chopped his face in two; then the top of his head lobbed backward, much as the hinged lid of the box containing her daughter's ashes had done, and he collapsed in a gory heap on her beautiful black-and-silver carpet.

"*Madame la reine,*" gasped the liveried villein who had smirked at her daughter's remains.

For him, she conjured a fireball and flung it at him. It landed in his hair. He shrieked for more minutes than she had care to listen.

So she swept from the Great Hall like the queen she was.

"And so, it falls to you," she said to the prostrate girl before her.

Three days had passed since Isabeau's death. It was in this very turret room that Isabeau had begged her to spare Jean de Deveraux, her new husband. Her huge, dark eyes had filled with tears, ignoring the warnings implicit in the entrails of the lambkin Catherine had sacrificed, begging for mercy for a man who would not grant her the same in return.

Because Isabeau was not yet with child, the Deveraux were planning to murder her in her marriage bed, thus to sever the alliance with the Cahors. The heads of both families had made an unspoken bargain: Isabeau would unite the houses by giving birth to a son if and when the Deveraux shared the secret of the Black Fire with the Cahors. Neither had been willing to go first; the stalemate had made Catherine impatient and Isabeau vulnerable. And so Catherine had laid siege to their castle and forced their hand.

"I knew it was a risk," she murmured, coming back to the present, and to the girl in front of her. "I knew that in all probability I would lose my daughter.

"And so, it falls to you," she repeated.

The girl was named Jeannette, which Catherine found propitious. Perhaps if Isabeau and the Deveraux prince had made a girl, they would have named her thus. This Jeannette was one of the bastard children of Catherine's first husband, Louis. He had many of them, but Jeannette carried within her blood the strongest magic of the male line. Long ago it was a witch who had brought strong blood to the Cahors line, and magical power was more pronounced in Cahors daughters than in sons, just as Deveraux sons carried their family's powers from generation to generation.

Jeannette had Louis's golden hair and quicksilver eyes; she was lithe and petite, a darling child of fourteen, and as she lay trembling before the great queen, she whispered, *"Je vous en prie, madame.* I am not worthy."

"You're afraid, and right to be," Catherine mused. "You're not well armed in the ways of the moon, and I have little time to prepare you for your role." *I should have had one waiting to step forward,* she thought. *That was an oversight, an incredible pride on my part.*

I assumed I would be able to protect Isabeau. I was so terribly, terribly wrong.

And now she is but dust. She is dead, and Jean is dead, and the two houses must both start over.

Catherine swept her skirts to her private altar.

Candles burned, and herbs; small doves huddled inside their cages, cowering as if they realized their fate. A golden statue of the Moon Lady, young, vibrant, and beautiful, stretched forth her arms to hold the libations Catherine had provided: ripe grain, wine, and the heart of a fine buck.

Seated atop the statue's head, preening and watchful, the lady hawk Pandion observed the proceedings. She cocked her head, her bells jingling, and fluttered her wings. Then she hunkered down to watch her mistress make magic.

Catherine grabbed one of the doves and stabbed it with the athame she held in her left hand. The warm blood gushed over her hand and onto the head of Jeannette, who gasped but said nothing.

Two more times Catherine anointed her with blood, then blessed the wine and gave it to Jeannette to drink. It was redolent with herbs designed to strengthen the girl's powers, and when Jeannette's head rolled back and her eyes lolled, unseeing, Catherine whispered spells over her for hours, hoping against hope that this young, untried girl would become a suitable heiress for her own mantle as High Priestess of the Cahors Coven.

And so began her work on Jeannette.

The young witchling was never allowed to leave the turret room. She wasn't yet strong enough to fight the magical influences of the Deveraux, who were surely plotting revenge. Catherine's spies had told her that Jean's place had been taken by one Paul, and that he was mighty and bold . . . but no Jean de Deveraux.

Moons passed, nearly six of them. Jeannette was practically half-mad from being locked up in the turret, and began to speak of visions she was having of the dead Isabeau, whose spirit would not rest.

Catherine was delighted to hear that her child had not yet departed for higher realms; that Isabeau was earthbound made her wonder if she could revive her, perhaps pour her soul into this little vessel. Never mind that such an act would no doubt cause the death of Jeannette's own soul. She was a bastard, and so far she had done nothing to fan any flames of warmth in her new mistress's heart.

The queen of the castle spent long hours casting spells and runes in order to contact her dead daughter. She made untold sacrifices. She raged, she pleaded with the Goddess . . . and she went unheard.

Finally she went to Jeannette, humiliated that such a chit could manage what she could not.

"My daughter. What stops her rest?" Catherine demanded of her.

"I . . . I don't know," Jeannette said miserably. "I

only see her in my mind, and know that she's not happy."

"Not *happy*?" Happiness was a foreign concept to Catherine. What on earth did happiness have to do with anything of import? Happiness was a sop to those who had no power, no fortune. There was no such thing, but rulers and bishops said so to keep the serfs and villeins in their traces.

"She is not happy," Jeannette repeated. And then she murmured, "And neither am I. Oh, stepmother, please let me leave this room!"

"You're not ready," Catherine insisted.

"I am! Oh, I beg of you, I am!" Jeannette threw herself on her knees and clasped Catherine around the legs. "I am going mad!"

Catherine touched the crown of Jeannette's hair, then moved firmly away. "Patience, girl. Soon. Soon you will have the wings you need to fly with Pandion." She smiled at the bird, who screeched at her in return.

But alas, Jeannette could not wait. Four moons later, Catherine learned that she had bribed one of the male servants to unlock the turret room, slipped out, and run to the forest to commune with the spirits. She had danced for hours, skyclad, then snuck back, put on her clothes, and pretended that nothing had happened.

This happened each moon for the next three moons.

Catherine's fury was matched only by her anxiety when the bishop arrived from Toulouse, as he did upon occasion, and with great unease, asked to speak to Catherine "of divers unsavory accusations against your ward."

Cahors was on the route from the wine valley to Toulouse; it seemed that travelers overnighting in the forest had witnessed Jeannette's pavane to the Goddess, and reported it to their priest. More rumors flew; soon the town was mumbling against the Cahors, calling them witches as they had done in the past.

There were prelates who knew the truth about the Cahors and the Deveraux, and others who did not. Each generation of French Coventry went about handling the Church as efficiently as possible. It had fallen to Catherine to be saddled with a virtuous Christian man who agreed wholeheartedly with the burnings that had been raging all over the continent.

"Of course you can understand my concern, *madame*," the bishop said to Catherine, as they walked in Catherine's beautiful rose garden. Isabeau's ashes had been buried there, and now a beautiful lily— symbol of the House of Cahors—drew nutrients from her mortal remains. "If such an abomination has found lodging in your family, that is to say, in your own bosom." He colored. "To turn a phrase."

"To turn a phrase," she said, "my husband's bastard is my concern, not yours."

The old man held up a finger. "All the souls in Christendom are the Church's concern, my daughter."

In the end, Catherine angrily capitulated and gave the prelate what he wanted. She herself denounced Jeannette, claiming to have seen her flying on a broomstick, and the bishop's guards dragged her screaming from the turret room, which had been stripped bare of all witchly trappings far in advance of their entry. A crucifix hung on the wall with a statue of the Madonna. Gone was Catherine's altar, and the bloodstains of the many sacrifices, and the arcana of witchly pursuit.

And gone was Pandion . . . until Jeannette was tied to the stake in the Cathedral yard in Toulouse. And then the lady hawk of the Cahors wheeled above her head, capering in the currents of hot air as Catherine's hopes, once more, burned to ash.

THREE

DEAD MOON

☾

In the night we dance and laugh
As our foes taste our wrath
Death we are and death we bring
Delivered on a falcon's wing

We dance upon each dead man's corpse
Laugh and shout till we grow hoarse
We treasure all our enemies' moans
As lady hawk talons crush their bones

Jer: The Island of Avalon

"You're going to live after all, *mon frère sorcier*," a voice said.

Jer couldn't tell where it was coming from. He tried to open his eyes; they were bandaged shut.

He couldn't move—or rather, he had no idea if he was able to move, or moving his body already. Agony permeated his being; he had no sense of a self beyond the pain that wracked him.

His father used to debate the notion of eternal torment with a warlock friend. Michael had held with the common belief that after a time, the victim would stop feeling the torture; that any sort of sensation, be it ecstatic bliss or the burning, scorching sensations that plagued Jer now, would become meaningless. The body would simply stop responding to them.

That was so wrong.

Pain begins in the mind, Jer thought, *and even my mind was burned. I am completely, utterly destroyed.*

Holly, he called out in his desperation, *save me. You can make it stop. You have the power.*

In a strange delirium he had dreamed of her; he had sat imprisoned in a room, shackled as a lure for her. He had begged her to stay away from him, as well he should do now. His family was covenanted to kill her.

She has a better chance if Eli died from his burns. Fantasme's spirit materialized and rescued him, but I pray to the God that the Black Fire killed him . . . more quickly than I seem to be dying.

He is evil, true, but he is my brother.

I can't wish this kind of pain on anyone.

Then a voice—the same voice—whispered in his ear again, "You're going to live."

He knew that voice; it was a part of him, an undying piece of his own soul. It was the voice of Jean de

Deveraux, the son of the House of Deveraux when the Cahors perpetrated the massacre upon Castle Deveraux.

"I did not die, either," Jean assured him. "They all believed that I died in the fire, but I survived. I told no one. I escaped with a small band of followers, and I stayed out of sight.

"I survived, and carried my warlock bloodline through my heirs in France to England and Montreal, and then to the Wild West.

"And you're going to survive, too, and kill my love," Jean continued, whispering in Jer's mind. "You shall kill Isabeau. And then she shall rest, and I will rest as well, because I will have my revenge at last."

Then another voice said, "You're going to live," and this one came from outside Jer's mind. "You will live, and you will join your father in his scheme to overthrow mine."

It's James, Jer realized. *The heir to the Moore Coven and son of Sir William, who is the leader of the Supreme Coven. Our family has secretly allied with James.*

That had been their original stance. But after Jer had been burned, Michael had pledged Jer to the service of Sir William in return for Jer's life. Upon sealing the bargain, Sir William had transformed into a hideous demon. *Is he a devil? Did my father make a deal with Satan himself so that I could survive?*

Suddenly the pain lessened, and Jer gasped with relief.

"It hurts, the Black Fire, doesn't it?" James murmured. "That's why we want the secret. The Supreme Coven wants this weapon so we can finally wipe out those idiot witches in the Mother Coven."

Jer was confused. Surely his father had already shared the secret. No way would Sir William let him hold a trump card like that.

"I can practically read your mind," James drawled. "Something has gone wrong, Jer. Your father can't conjure the Black Fire anymore. We have no idea why he continues to fail."

Jer was taken aback.

"I think it's because he needs you and Eli both, that there must be three Deveraux present to make the fire burn. With you out of commission and away from him, it isn't working. My father thinks I'm wrong. He thinks that bitch Holly is blocking it. So my father sent him home to kill her.

"What about you, Jer? Would you kill her if I ordered you to? You're with me, or you're against me. You're going to get well, and you, your father, and your brother, are going to conjure the Black Fire for me."

Eli must be alive, Jer thought, and he was both dismayed and relieved at the thought. *I still care about him.*

Blood is thicker than water after all . . . warlock blood, that is. . . .

"Sit up," James commanded him.

Magic thrummed through Jer Deveraux, binding up seared flesh; reopening veins that had melted shut; clearing the scars from his lungs and his heart. His breathing came more freely; he sucked in both air and magic, and the glow pulsated and spread throughout his body, expelling with his exhalations. He was dizzy, almost high, and then the pain was almost gone. *Almost, but not quite.*

Then Jer found himself seated in a wheelchair on a cliff, facing out to sea. Magical energy swirled and undulated around him, motes of green phosphorescence danced over his skin.

His skin, which was black and shriveled and repulsive.

He stared in horror at his hands, dangling loosely in his lap. They were charred stumps, bones poking through the lumps of cindered flesh. A witch at the stake would have looked no worse.

I'm a monster, like Sir William. Maybe he was burned by the Black Fire too. Maybe my father conjured it before, years ago, and Sir William bears the scars.

Tears rolled down his face. His body shook with grief and rage and deep, abject humiliation.

I can never let Holly see me like this. She'd pull away,

probably throw up. I couldn't take that.

"You begin to understand what the Cahors are capable of," said Jean de Deveraux's voice inside Jer's head. *"Eh, bien,* that's what I looked like too, after my wife betrayed me. And why I both love and loathe my Isabeau. And why you must kill the reigning Cahors witch, who is known as Holly Cathers. My Isabeau can possess her and she has betrayed us both now. So they must die, the one with the other."

"No," Jer croaked. He had no idea how long it had been since he had spoken a word. "Holly did not betray me."

"But she did," Jean insisted. *"La femme* Holly, she knew that bound together, Deveraux and Cahors— *pardon, on dit* 'Cathers'—could stay untouched within the flame of the Black Fire that your family conjured last Beltane. By holding on to each other, you both could have stood inside the flames for an entire moon, had you so desired.

"But she moved away from you in the fire, did she not? *Mon ami,* she abandoned you to the flames, as Isabeau swore to do to me, knowing full well that you would suffer like this."

"Her cousins dragged her away!" Jer rasped. "She had no choice."

"How pathetic, that you lie so poorly to yourself,"

Jean said contemptuously. "She's the strongest witch in the Cahors line since Catherine, Isabeau's mother. If she had really wanted to save you, she could have."

"No," Jer whispered, but he had no rebuttal; deep in his sizzling, superheated Deveraux soul, he believed what Jean was saying.

Then he had another vision: He was standing on the shoreline in Seattle, with Holly; the waves flung themselves against their ankles, and then their calves, and their knees. But his arms were around Holly, and she was kissing him deeply, her entire body pressed against his. She was hungry for him, and so eager. . . .

. . . and the waves crashed around them, and crashed; Holly held him tightly and kept her mouth over his. The chill waters yanked at them and tugged hard.

They tumbled out to sea, caught up in the cresting waves and the chasms between them. Jer fought, trying to keep his head above the rollercoaster of water, but Holly clung to him and pulled him down, down; her mouth was over his and he couldn't draw a breath. She had effectively cut off all his oxygen. In his panic and frustration, he tried to break free, but he couldn't. She was drowning him.

"She will be the death of you, if you don't kill her first," Jean whispered. "Isabeau is bound to take my life, through you if she must. She cannot rest until I am obliterated."

And then James spoke, as if he were part of this vision, as if he lived both outside and inside Jer's mind:

"Remember who your friends are, Deveraux," James added.

Jean continued. "And never, ever forget your enemies. In the lives of witch and warlock, blood feuds go on for centuries. *Mademoiselle* Holly may want to love you, may even be able to convince herself that she does; but she is the living embodiment of all that is Cahors, and she is your mortal enemy."

Holly and Amanda: Seattle, October

It was a very dark and stormy night, nearly Samhain, and Uncle Richard was drunk.

Holly and Amanda had just gotten home from Circle, both taking off their cloaks of invisibility to find him sitting in the living room in the dark, compulsively eating the miniature chocolate bars purchased for trick-or-treaters, straight out of the bag. He didn't even pretend anymore; he was drinking Scotch straight out of the bottle. In the early days after Aunt Marie-Claire's death, he had mixed drinks for himself, making them progressively stronger; then he had taken to drinking out of a shot glass. That was before he had

had proof that Marie-Claire had been having an affair with Michael Deveraux.

Poor Uncle Richard had discovered the truth in a horribly prosaic way: Marie-Claire had kept a diary, and Richard found it. She had written of her nights with Michael in unstinting detail and Richard had read every word.

"Daddy?" Amanda asked gently as she knelt by his chair.

He sighed and ticked his gaze to her, his eyes rheumy and bloodshot. There was a week's growth of beard on his face. He smelled.

She and Holly had not been able to talk Richard into moving away. He was determined to fall apart in his own home. Since he didn't work anymore, letting his business die day by day, week by week, it had proven to be a challenge to ward and protect the house while he was around. But the coven had managed it. He was relatively safe . . . or to be completely frank, in as much danger as the others.

"Uncle Richard?" Holly queried. She moved her hand and blessed him. He didn't seem to notice the furtive hand gesture, and it didn't seem to make him any better.

"I'll make you some coffee." Amanda brushed past Holly and went into the kitchen.

Holly took up the vigil next to Uncle Richard's chair. She put her hand on his and said, "I'm so sorry."

He turned his head and stared at her; and in the dim light of the moon, she saw that his eyes had rolled up in his head. Startled, she drew away.

But he caught her hand and held it tightly, nearly crushing the bones. His voice eked out, weird and disembodied, as he said, in Michael Deveraux's voice, *"Die soon, Holly Cathers.*

"Die horribly."

Nicole: Spain, October

As they crept down the streets of Madrid, Philippe kept close to Nicole, obviously eager to be near her, perhaps more intent on keeping her safe. He was a rock, and she was grateful for his strength and his interest in keeping close by; for the first time in a long while she felt safe. He was not as dramatically handsome as José Luís, who had wild Gypsy blood in his veins. He was more like her Amanda: pleasing to look at, but not startling. The extremes of looks and emotions were left to others of their covens: in Amanda's case, Nicole tended to steal the show; in Philippe's, it was José Luís.

Philippe did stand out from his coven, though, in that he wasn't Spanish. He was from Agen, a small town in France.

Now he spoke to their leader, saying, "José Luís, we need to leave the streets. It's not safe tonight, not even for us."

"*Tienes razón,*" José Luís agreed. He raised his voice so that the others could clearly hear him, "Come, we go."

They had been together for several days, keeping on the run, finding safe houses that José Luís and his lieutenant, Philippe, had set up long ago. They were warriors in the cause of White Magic, and they had many enemies. Philippe told her that something had been tracking them before she had arrived, but she had the feeling that her presence was like a homing beacon, pointing the way to their coven.

Alicia, the witch Philippe had silenced, had left the coven, jealous of Nicole and irritated that she had been charmed when she'd spoken against her.

José Luís was the tallest of the group, and the best dressed. He was wearing black leather pants and a black-washed silk shirt. His curly hair fell past his shoulders, and he had casually pulled it back and secured it in a ponytail with an elastic band he took from his pocket. From his features she would have guessed his age to be about thirty, but his eyes looked older, *much* older.

Philippe, who appeared a few years younger, had

swarthy skin and bright green eyes, a startling combination in contrasts. He wore jeans and sweaters against the cold of the Madrid autumn, expensively tooled cowboy boots, and, on occasion, a cowboy hat. His chestnut hair was cut short, very stylish, and on the one occasion that she had touched it, she was startled by how silky it felt to her touch.

Though he was usually jovial, now he was all business.

He feels it too, she thought.

José Luís had introduced the oldest member of his coven as "Señor Alonzo, our benefactor, our father figure."

Alonzo had snorted in derision, but extended his hand to Nicole. She had clasped it, and in one smooth movement he twisted her hand so that he could kiss the top of it. He released it easily and stepped back. Everything about the man bespoke grace and elegance.

Armand was their "conscience," José Luís had told her. His dark eyes crackled and his mouth was set in a hard line. There was something dark and dangerous about him, as if he were a villain from some old-time movie.

Pablo was José Luís's younger brother. He looked younger than Nicole herself, perhaps fourteen, and he was very shy.

At the time she had met them all, she had thought, *What a motley assortment!*

And Pablo had replied quietly, in heavily accented English, "But we get the job done."

Startled, Nicole had stared at him. Philippe chuckled. "Pablo is gifted in ways that are beyond the rest of us." The boy just blushed harder and continued to stare down at his shoes.

"And who are you?" José Luís had asked at last.

It was her turn to blush. "My name is Nicole Anderson. I'm just . . . I'm . . . visiting Spain."

"You're a long way from your home," Jose observed, scrutinizing her. "And you are of the witch blood. I sincerely doubt, *mi hermosa,* that you are . . . *visiting* Spain."

She nodded, tears stinging her eyes.

"I'm . . . I'm in trouble," she managed. "Big trouble."

"Warlock trouble," Pablo filled in.

Nicole nodded. She had no idea if she should tell them what was going on; she worried that she might endanger them. "I . . . I'm so scared."

José Luís smoothed over the moment. "*Está bien. No te precupes, bruja.* You will be safe with us. You can be part of our coven."

"But I don't want to be part of a coven," she heard herself protesting.

José Luís had laughed. "It's a little late for that."

And that had been when Philippe stepped forward and said, "I will watch out for you, Nicole."

And he had, ever since. It was he who conjured wards around her to deflect magical seeking spells; and he who made sure she had enough to eat when they stopped for meals; and he who watched her in the night as she bedded down, studying the air around her, making sure she never slept close to a window.

He, who had obviously begun to care for her . . .

. . . and she for him.

Now, on the dusty streets of Madrid, the sense of being hunted grew stronger with the darkness. Tonight, Nicole's senses were screaming that some-one—or something—was gaining on them, fast.

"Philippe is right. I think we should leave," Pablo announced. "It's become too dangerous here. We can go to the French border. We have friends there."

The others began to murmur, quietly assenting.

Nicole shook her head and stepped back, pulling her hand from Philippe's grasp. "I can't go with you. I'll . . . I just want to go home. I shouldn't have left in the first place." In a tiny voice she added, "It was very cowardly of me."

He nodded sympathetically. "I understand, but that is not possible at the moment. When it is safe, we will do what we can to see you home."

"All the way to Seattle?" she croaked.

His grin broadened. "Yes, even all the way to Seattle." He clapped his hands. *"Bueno, andale,"* he said to the rest of the coven. *"La noche esta demasiado peligroso." The night is too dangerous.*

Several of the covenate made the sign of the cross. Nicole was startled and about to ask about it when the band began to move.

As if of a single mind, they slunk through the center of Madrid, turning down side streets as one, never speaking, never hesitating. As though in a dream, Nicole allowed herself to be swept along with the five cloaked figures. Philippe once again had her by the hand, and she found herself half trotting to keep up with his long strides.

An hour passed before they finally stopped in an alley beside a small car. Nicole hesitated as the others climbed in. Philippe smiled at her.

"We are safe. For the moment."

Nicole nodded slowly, staring from him to the car. His smile began to fade, and he glanced at the shadows whence they had come.

"I sense that there is not much time," he said. "We must go now if we are to escape. Do you feel it?"

She nodded. "Yes," she said unhappily. "I do."

It felt as if someone were staring down at them from a great height—like a huge, winged creature preparing to take flight, flap its enormous wings, and pluck all of them up with its razor-sharp talons. She could almost hear an eerie, echoic screech.

The falcon, she thought. *He's coming.*

Philippe urged Nicole into the car. "This is an old Deux Chevaux," he told her. "A French car. We call them 'two horses' because that's all the horsepower they have." He grinned. "But even a Deux Chevaux beats something made in Spain."

"Tiene cuidado, macho," José Luís said with mock menace.

"Tais-toi!" Philippe shot back. He gave Nicole a quick wink and a smile. "You see? Even in danger, we can joke and insult one another. We are a strong band, Nicole. We will be all right."

She tried to smile back, but her anxiety was rising with each heartbeat. She found herself in the front seat wedged between José Luís and Philippe.

"Um, seat belt," she murmured, fumbling for the straps.

"It is okay. I am a good driver," Philippe informed her with a crooked smile.

She nodded grimly.

"We cannot go back for our belongings," Philippe told her. "Do you have your passport? Your money and things like that?"

She patted her pockets and nodded. "Yes." She had brought very few things with her, but she was sorry to give them up. She felt so . . . naked with nothing to change into. *And no shampoo. No toothbrush.*

Pablo leaned forward and said something to Philippe, who murmured, "Ah, *sí*," and turned to Nicole. "We'll buy new things," he said kindly. "Once we are safe."

Three hours later they pulled up to a villa just as dawn broke behind it, the light dancing on the white walls of the low, sprawling country house. Flowers edged a cobbled path to the front door.

The sight took Nicole's breath away.

It's too beautiful to be dangerous, she thought, knowing in her heart that that didn't make any sense.

José Luís stepped out of the car and Nicole moved to follow him, but Philippe laid a hand on her arm, stopping her. "Best to let him go alone. He needs to, how do you say, make a check?"

Nicole peered out the window and watched as a tall man left the villa and approached José Luís. The two men strode toward each other purposefully, each swaggering slightly. When they got within fifteen feet of each other they began shouting. She couldn't understand the words, but they didn't sound friendly.

The men stopped when they stood nearly toe-to-toe. They were gesturing wildly and seemed to be arguing even more heatedly. At last José Luís threw back his head and laughed. The other man did as well, and then they embraced.

At last they broke apart and José Luís returned to the car, a smile stretching his sharp features. He gestured for everyone to join him, and as Nicole stepped from the car she shook her head in bewilderment.

"What was that all about?" she asked him.

"Just a little family reunion," José Luís answered with a sparkle in his eye.

Nicole flipped her hair back over her shoulders and decided not to question him further. *At least not about that,* she thought. She fell into step with Philippe as José Luís led the group around the house.

About half a mile behind the villa there was a small cottage, which was, apparently, their safe house. When they reached it, José Luís confidently opened the door and ushered them all inside. The place was small but clean; several cots lined the walls.

Nicole's eyelids felt heavy and the crisp white sheets looked cool and inviting.

I am so tired, she thought. *Tired of running. Tired of worrying.*

Wearily she sat down on a chair and slipped off her heavy-soled shoes. Her jeans were dusty. Philippe had given her a sweatshirt that read UNI DE MADRID, and that was dirty too. Her mouth was gritty; when José Luís went to a small cabinet, opened it, and brought out a bottle of wine, she accepted a swig along with the others and used it to rinse out the bad taste. Then someone volunteered that there was soap and shampoo in the bathroom.

"Mujer," Philippe said to her, "go and have a, how do you say, a soak?"

The wine had gone to her head; she felt a little fuzzy as she blurted excitedly, "There's a bathtub? Really? Are you . . . it's okay?"

He gestured to the cottage. "It's heavily protected. This may be the only chance you have for some while." He grinned at her and added, "A beautiful woman such as you should have some pleasures."

She blinked; warmth coiled in her lower belly and spread, and she felt the heat rising in her cheeks. He took her hand and raised it to his lips.

He's thinking about me in the tub, she thought.

As he pulled off his boots, Pablo glanced up at her, reddened, and looked away.

So is he.

Not for the first time, she became very aware that she was now the only female in the coven. The other witch, Alicia, had not been very welcomed to begin with, and no one had been sorry to see her go. And yet these men were not precisely warlocks, not in the same violent, harsh way as Eli and his father. They were male witches.

It's more like Eddie, Kialish, and Kialish's father, she thought. *It's a different thing. I wonder what Holly and Amanda would think about that. Maybe Jer's a male witch too. Maybe that's why he always had so much trouble fitting in as a Deveraux.*

It was strange. She knew that once, not long before, she would have made the most of the opportunity and basked in the attention of five men. She felt herself blushing and stole a glance at Philippe. All that seemed a long time past. There was only one man she really wanted attention from now.

Rummaging in the cabinets, Armand, the quiet, serious one, said something to José Luís, who in turn cocked his head questioningly at Nicole.

"Armand asks, are you Catholic?"

"No." She frowned at him, gazing past him at Armand. "Are you?"

"We're Spanish." He chuckled. "*Bueno,* Philippe is

French, but *sí,* we are all Catholic. In fact, we call Armand our 'conscience' because he was once a student of the priesthood. He wishes to conduct a Mass for us." José Luís smiled reassuringly as her lips parted in astonishment. "A white Mass, not a black one."

"But . . ." She hesitated. "We pray to the Goddess."

José Luís shrugged. "It's all the same, Nicolita. But what I am thinking is, it would be better if you took your soak. We who are of the faith will say our Mass."

"All . . . all right."

Señor Alonzo held up a finger, saying something to José Luís. He looked puzzled.

Then Philippe said, "Towels," and the others nodded. To Nicole, he explained, "They were trying to remember the word in English." He smiled at her. "They want you to know there are fresh towels in the bath."

"Thank you. *Gracias,*" she attempted. Smiles broke out all around.

Self-consciously she made her way into the bathroom. She found a light switch to her left and flicked it on.

A beautiful claw-foot tub sat to her right, and there was a small partition for the toilet and sink basin. She found the dark purple towels in a cupboard above the toilet, a bottle of what seemed to be shampoo, and a thick, fragrant bar of Maja soap wrapped in paper embossed with a picture of a flamenco dancer.

Breathing in the delicious perfume, she carried everything to the tub and turned on the double spigots. The tub was clean; she guessed that the man who had greeted José Luís so oddly kept the safe house clean in the event that it was needed. She was grateful for that. She was doubly grateful for Philippe's kindness in suggesting she take a bath.

Kindness? She smirked at herself. *Face it, Nicki. There's something there and you both feel it.*

There was a rubber stopper in the bottom of the tub; she plugged the drain and let the water run. Her head bobbed as she waited, and she thought, *I'll have to be careful. I could fall asleep in here.*

From the other room, a single male voice sang out in a rising, falling chant. The others echoed it. Then the first voice sang again, and the others responded.

They're chanting.

From deep inside her, ancient blood called to the rhythm, the mournful, gentle melodies. Part of her knew these words, these notes; it was in her blood, in her spirit, and in her soul.

The Cahors lived in a Catholic country. Does my spirit stretch back that far, like Holly's does?

Pondering, she peeled off her dirty clothes and

stepped cautiously into the bath. Easing her sore body down into the warm water, she moaned under her breath as aching muscles uncoiled. She couldn't remember the last time she had actually relaxed.

She lay back and closed her eyes, listening to the chanting. Her mind began to drift. . . . She thought of happier days, when Mom was alive, the two of them having just discovered magic. They had started blessing the family every evening, and Nicole had hoped that her mom would stop sleeping with Michael; that she, Nicole, could light a spark between her parents and they would love each other.

And that I could make Eli good. . . .

I loved him.

Tears slid down her face as she finally let go and allowed herself to feel some of her grief. Her mother was dead.

I miss Amanda. And Holly. And my cat. Oh, how I miss Hecate.

And then she was drifting along . . . drifting and bobbing . . . on water . . . *down a river; she was the Lady of the Island, and she dare not see the imprisoned one; if she looked on him she would go mad because he was so hideous. . . .*

"Nicki . . . ," came a voice. "Nicki, where are you? My father is sending the falcon to find you. Let me find you first."

"Eli?" she slurred. Her body was so heavy; her

head weighed a ton. She was aware that she was slipping lower into the water, the beautiful river that wound past the island . . . where . . . Jer . . .

"Nicki?"

She sank slowly, like Ophelia, with holly and lilies twined in her hair. Down, deeply down, the water caressing her chin; then down again, to her lower lip . . .

Drifting along as men sang holy words, and Eli whispered at her . . .

. . . and the waters met over her upper lip. Through her eyelids, in a magical way, she became aware that someone was standing beside the tub, and saying to her in a language she didn't speak, but in the ways of dreams and enchantments, she could understand, "Wake up, Nicole. Wake up, or you will die."

But Nicole couldn't move. A strange lassitude had overtaken her. She let herself slide deeper into the water. . . . It was so warm, so inviting . . . and she was so very, very tired . . .

. . . of living. . . .

The woman's soft voice said fearfully, in the same lilting foreign language—*it's Old French,* Nicki realized—"The curse is water. . . ."

FOUR

SNOW MOON

☾

Prepare now, House of Deveraux
To wreak vengeance on all our foes
Careful now as we plan the worst
Think and scheme, pray and curse

We huddle together beneath the skies
Their darkness reflected in our eyes
Rest and plot the overthrow
Of the House of Deveraux

Holly and Amanda: Seattle, October

Holly and Amanda took turns watching over Uncle
Richard as he collapsed into a drunken stupor and
began to snore. They had no idea what to do with him,
and they called Tante Cecile on her cell phone for help.
She had come over immediately, with Silvana in tow.

The voodoo priestess had called upon the *loa,* the
gods, who could also possess people, and they advised
her to keep him locked in his bedroom until a full

exorcism could be conducted. As Richard had no witch blood in his veins, Tante Cecile assumed that Michael had been able to possess him because he had been weakened by drink. It was a known fact in occult circles that people in altered states of consciousness were easier to invade than those who kept their wits about them. Those of the old traditions—the Druids, the pagans, shaman, Orphic Mystery cultists, and even ancient Christians—willingly relinquished themselves for the use of their spirits and gods through potent herbs, fasting, and even pain.

But Richard was another matter.

"Michael could try to force him to hurt you," Tante Cecile told them as she sat with her daughter, Amanda, and Holly in the living room.

Amanda nodded dully. Holly's heart went out to her. She'd been through so much.

Then her cousin muttered, "He's already hurt us. He stood by while Mom . . . She needed someone stronger."

Holly traded shocked looks with Silvana. "Amanda, you're not blaming your dad for your mom's . . . that she went to Michael Deveraux." She couldn't bring herself to say the word "affair."

Silvana chimed in. "For heaven's sake, Amanda, Michael Deveraux bewitched your mother!"

Amanda balled her fists. "He didn't need to bewitch her. She would've . . ." She took a deep breath. "Daddy doesn't know this, but Michael wasn't the first."

"Oh, Mandy, no," Holly said softly.

"Yes. *Yes.*" She touched her fingertips to her forehead. "I found her other diaries right after the funeral. I read them, and then I burned them. But Daddy got to her most recent one before I could. That was the one about Michael."

The others were speechless. Holly thought back to her parents and how unhappy they'd been together. *Did either one of them cheat?*

She couldn't bear the thought.

Suddenly a trio of stricken yowls pierced the silence. It was the cats, howling in terror, the three flashing down the stairs and racing into the living room, where Bast deposited a dead bird at Holly's feet. It was about two feet long, far too large for a cat Bast's size to bring down, very black and shiny. A trickle of blood dribbled onto the carpet from its breast. As it lay on its side, one lifeless eye glared up at Holly.

As Amanda and Silvana jumped to their feet, Tante Cecile bent over the cat's gory trophy and murmured an incantation. From her jeans pocket she pulled a chicken claw and gestured at the air above the body, then around it. Silvana joined her; they were speaking a language Holly didn't know, but she took Amanda's hand and said, "Within, without, our wards hold. The circle cannot fall."

Amanda joined in. "Witchly sisters are we, strong of spirit, stout of heart; we demand protection from the Goddess; we are her moon children."

There was a sudden flurry in the chimney, as if of birds trying to fly out; Bast leaped into Holly's lap, raised up on her back legs, and put her paws on Holly's chest. Her yellow eyes stared into Holly's. Holly stared back. Hecate mewed plaintively, over and over and over again.

A chill crept through the room; Holly almost felt a hand on her shoulder and jumped slightly. Tante Cecile eyed her carefully and said, "She is with us."

"She?" Holly asked.

Tante Cecile stared at Amanda, who glanced around the room and cried out, "Mom?"

"No, Amanda," Tante Cecile said sadly. "Isabeau."

Holly swallowed. Amanda nodded, disappointed but focused on the task at hand, and took a deep breath. She murmured, "Blessed be."

"Blessed be," Holly added.

Tante Cecile said, "Ignore the bird, girls. Make a circle with me."

The trio moved away from the sofa and closer to the fireplace. As Tante Cecile bent down and placed logs on the andiron, she turned to Holly and said, "Make a fire, honey. It's cold."

Holly nodded. She found a place inside herself and filled it with the heat and color of fire, imagining it, seeing orange, yellow, and red flames, smelling the smoke. She said in Latin, *"Succendo aduro!"* and the fire ignited.

No one was surprised. Holly had been able to start fires for months. Black Fire was another story.

I don't know what one has to be or do to be able to conjure that, she thought, *and I'm not sure I want to know.*

Though the others brightened at the sight of the fire, Holly felt no warmth from it. She was getting colder, and the chill was seeping into her bones.

Amanda said to her, "Holly, there's a blue glow around your head."

The others nodded. "I see it too," Silvana said.

She looked down at her hands; they were not glowing. Then all of a sudden it was as if someone had drilled a little hole in the center of her skull and poured chilled pudding into it. The sensation seeped through her head, giving her a cold headache and half-freezing her face in place. She felt slowed down—her breathing, her heartbeat, her thoughts. She became aware that the other three had grouped around her and someone pushed her gently into a chair. Then they placed their hands on her head and Tante Cecile began to speak in French.

Holly felt herself answering, also in French.

"Je suis . . . Isabeau."

Then Holly lost track of what was going on; she was vaguely aware of the outer world, but her attention was being forced on an image she saw with her mind's eye: a beautiful woman—her ancestress, Isabeau—locked in a passionate embrace with Jer . . . no, not Jer Deveraux, but his ancestor, Jean, husband to Isabeau . . . *they're in their marriage bed. . . . The hangings are red and green, the colors of the Deveraux; mistletoe and oak and ivy twine everywhere; it's like a forest; there are herbs burning in the fireplace for fertility. The moon is full; her heart is full, and so is his. They have enchanted each other; passion has ignited; they are in desperate love . . . not expected . . . not welcomed . . .*

". . . though we couple," Isabeau thought inside Holly's head, *"we are mortal enemies, fully prepared to murder one another in this very bed; if he does not . . ."*

And then the image blurred, as if someone had changed a channel.

Now Holly was standing in a strange bathroom,

calmly looking down at Nicole, whose head had just sunk beneath the water. Bubbles sputtered on the surface.

"*Aidez . . . la Nicole,*" Isabeau said inside her mind. "I tried to wake her, but she cannot hear me. She will be able to hear you, Holly. Wake her up!"

More bubbles trickled upward to the surface.

"Nicole!" she shouted aloud. "Nicole, wake up!"

Nicole's head shot up from the water; she looked around, startled.

The cold sensation immediately dissipated, and Holly became aware of the other three women, whose faces were filled with concern.

"What about her? What's wrong?" Amanda cried. "Where's my sister?"

"Isabeau," Tante Cecile commanded, "speak to us."

There was no reply. The room was warm to her, and she felt alone and very dizzy.

Isabeau had left.

Holly said, "It's just me now." She took a deep breath and told them what she had seen.

Amanda grabbed Holly's shoulders. Her face was contorted with fear, her features constricted while her eyes were huge.

"Nicole woke up, right? She's okay?"

"As far as I could tell," Holly said honestly.

"No clues about where she was?" Tante Cecile queried.

Holly shook her head. "I'm sorry. It was just a bathroom."

"Don't be sorry," Silvana put in. Her silver beads flashed in the firelight as she shook her head. "You probably saved Nicole's life."

Holly nodded. "I feel that. I'm certain that I did." She gestured at the dead bird, pointed at it, and murmured a quick spell of levitation. As if by invisible hands, the inert bird lifted into the air and floated to the fireplace. Then it was flung with contempt into the fire.

It burst into flame and was instantly consumed.

Then one by one, the cats walked to them, joining their circle: Holly's cat, Bast; Amanda's beloved Freya; and Nicole's Hecate. All three named for goddesses, all three more than cats.

"Blessings on you, Bast," Holly said. "You caught an enemy."

The cat blinked up at her and began to purr. The other two sat on their haunches beside Bast, and stared up expectantly at Holly.

"Your familiars," Tante Cecile told her, "are waiting for you to tell them what to do."

Holly and Amanda looked first at each other and

then at the cats. Amanda said, "Patrol the house. Kill any enemies that you find."

Holly said to her cousin, "That's a good idea. And we should also—"

A sharp contraction rippled through her. Her eyes rolled back in her head, and she collapsed.

She began to jerk uncontrollably, arms and legs flailing. She heard Amanda shouting her name, heard Silvana and her aunt crying out in French.

Then she was struggling under rip-current waters rushing everywhere, tumbling her over. She was back in the Grand Canyon, reliving the accident, clutching at the straps that held her in the raft. She knew in her soul that nearby, her father was already dead, her mother had but seconds to live, and Tina was going to last longest of all, nearly an entire minute longer than Ryan, their river guide, who was losing consciousness at this moment. And she was drowning.

Then the blue glow materialized, as before, and took form as Isabeau, who floated toward her, her fingers nimbly working the buckles . . .

. . . and her voice filled Holly's mind once more: *It is the curse of the Cahors,* ma chere *Holly. Those who love us die not in flame, but by water. They die by water.*

It was the Deveraux who put that curse on us. They have hounded us through time, attempting to kill us off.

You must survive. We must end this vendetta . . . forever.

On the floor, Holly gasped for air, sucking it in hungrily, starved for it, and began to cough.

Tante Cecile patted her hard on the back; water spewed out of her mouth, and the other two girls cried out.

Amanda was beside her in an instant. She took Holly's hands in hers and said, "Your fingers are wet."

Holly blurted, "Amanda, there's a curse on us. People we love, they drown. It's the curse of the Cahors."

She buried her face in her hands. "I killed my parents with my witch blood. I killed them because I'm cursed!"

"Hush, now," Tante Cecile ordered her. "You didn't kill them."

"But it's real," Holly insisted, pulling her hands from her face and lifting her head. "Isabeau told me." She clutched at Amanda. "What do we do?"

"We use that knowledge, and we work with it," Tante Cecile cut in. Her face was filled with grim purpose. "Silvana, get a big bowl of water from their kitchen. If that's how they play, that's how we play. We are going to drown whatever is possessing Richard Anderson."

★ ★ ★

It was wild work, and it went by in a blur of nerves and exhaustion.

The four gathered in the bedroom, where they had bound an unconscious Uncle Richard to the bed. As Silvana lit candles and sounded a small gong, Tante Cecile chanted and talked to the *loa*. The cats joined in, howling. Then something dark floated out of him, and at Tante Cecile's instruction, Holly grabbed it with both hands and plunged it into the bowl of water.

It struggled in her hands and then went limp. She pulled her hands away, and it was a strange, tiny creature that reminded Holly of a cross between a frog and an elf.

"It's an imp," Tante Cecile said with satisfaction. "You killed it."

Holly nodded, near collapse. On Tante Cecile's instruction, she dragged herself off to bed.

Sleep came quickly to Holly, but the oblivion of rest was short-lived. Soon she was dreaming, and she was standing once more in the room with Jer. She tried to speak with him, but no words would come, and he lay, hunched over on his side, asleep. For a minute she watched the rise and fall of his chest, willing him to wake and to see her.

It was no use.

Suddenly a hand brushed against the back of her

neck. She jumped and turned around, heart racing, and prepared to fight.

A woman in a long white gown stood there. Red hair fell in waves all the way down to her knees. Her face was unearthly beautiful but with sad, haunting eyes that pierced Holly's soul.

She shook her head slowly as if to silence Holly's unspoken questions. Then she raised her hand and beckoned Holly to follow. Holly passed with her through the wall of the cell and then followed her for what seemed ages through twisting corridors lit only by sporadic torches.

Neither the woman's nor Holly's feet made any sound against the stone floors, and the silence unnerved her. At last Holly strained, trying to clear her throat, to make some sound to shatter the silence that overwhelmed her. Her throat felt constricted and she felt the fear growing in her. She had to speak, to say something. . . .

The woman turned and laid a pale finger against her ruby lips. Again she shook her head and slowly pointed toward a dark alcove in the wall. Holly could see nothing in the blackness and finally shook her head in frustration. The woman glided back toward her and gestured for Holly to close her eyes. When she did, the woman's fingers pressed gently on her eyelids.

When her touch was gone, Holly opened her eyes. Her vision was sharper, clearer, and within the alcove she saw two huge beasts staring with unblinking eyes right at her. She jerked backward, but the woman's hand was on her arm, steadying her. She pointed to the animals, then to her own eyes, and shook her head no.

Somehow the beasts couldn't see them, but what Holly saw of them terrified her. Both were as big as lions, though they had the general shape of dogs. Their eyes glowed red and their brown-black fur stood up all over their bodies coarse and unyielding as spines. Their fangs were three inches long and saliva dripped in a steady flow from their open mouths. *Hellhounds,* Holly thought as she shuddered. *They can't see me, but they might be able to hear me.*

The woman turned and began to move on, and Holly hurried to follow behind. At long last they passed into a room where the woman stopped. She turned slowly to Holly and moved her arm, as if displaying the room to her. Holly gazed about her, her newfound sight seeing everything in excruciating detail.

Bottles of strange-looking liquids lined musty shelves. Still more bottles and flasks littered each of six huge work tables. Ancient manuscripts written in half a dozen different languages lay open everywhere. In the middle of one table a tall pointed hat with stars on it sat in a prominent place.

She felt a smile break out on her face. It looked just like the hat Mickey wore as the Sorcerer's Apprentice. She strode forward to touch the hat, trying to hold in her laughter. Her fingers were an inch from it when the woman clasped her wrist hard.

Holly bit back a startled exclamation of pain as she looked at the other woman. A warning shone in her eyes as she shook her head fiercely. Puzzled, Holly turned back to look at the hat. The stars on it were suddenly alive, glowing and twisting about on the hat in a crazy kaleidoscope. Heat was pouring from its surface and Holly pulled her hand back quickly.

She stared in wonder as the hat slowly returned to the inanimate object it had been before. *What would have happened if I had actually touched it?* She could feel the power emanating from it now; she had been too amused by it earlier to notice. The woman half smiled at her before extending her hand toward one of the walls.

Holly followed her gaze to a weathered and water-stained hanging. It looked to be ancient parchment, or maybe it was leather, stippled with faded gray shapes and letters.

It's a map.

Excitement rippled through her.

She's trying to tell me where Jer is!

She scanned it; all the words were in Latin, and she didn't recognize the lay of the land at all. Frantic, she scrutinized the shapes and cursed her geography teacher for being so boring that Holly had slept through every class.

There!

There was a small island with an *X* over the top of it. She tapped it with her finger and glanced questioningly at the other woman as she glided over.

The apparition dipped her head in acknowledgment. Holly turned back to the map, searching desperately for something that she recognized. Another island, much larger, seemed to be close by; the shape of it tickled something in Holly's memory.

England! It has to be.

Triumphant, she turned back to the other woman, only to find her staring toward the wall opposite with a look of fear on her face.

Someone's coming. I can sense it too.

On the table, the hat began to glow. . . .

Her fear palpable, the woman waved her hand above her head, and everything turned black. Then someone burst into the room, bellowing, "Sasha!"

Holly screamed and bolted upright.

Amanda burst into her room, eyes wild, hair

sticking out in all directions. She grabbed Holly by the shoulders and shook her.

"Holly, are you all right?"

Holly managed to nod, composing herself, wiping tears from her eyes, swallowing around the tightness in her throat. Unable to speak, she motioned for a glass of water, and Amanda ran out of the room. Amanda was back in seconds with a Dixie cup from the bathroom. Holly downed the water gratefully, her throat finally loosening.

Finished with the water, Holly looked up at Amanda to tell her about her dream and strangled back a gasp. Amanda's face seemed huge to her. She could see every blemish in her cousin's skin, could clearly distinguish every strand of hair. She blinked fiercely, willing the enhanced sight away.

It remained. She groaned and sank back onto her pillow, squeezing her eyes shut.

"What is it?" Amanda asked, quieter now.

"I had a dream. There was a woman. Someone . . . a relative, I think."

Amanda sounded concerned. "Isabeau?"

Holly shook her head. "No. I don't know who she was. She took me to this room where there was an old map. I found this island on it and it was close to England."

Holly risked opening her eyes a bit. Amanda's expression was one of puzzlement.

"Wait right here," she murmured getting up again.

"Gladly," Holly answered, closing her eyes again. She felt sick and queasy, so disoriented that it was as if the bed were rocking. Almost unconsciously she reached for Bast, who rose from her haunches at the foot of the bed and sauntered toward her mistress.

Amanda was gone for several minutes. Holly began to drift. Bast slipped herself under Holly's arm and began to purr.

Holly felt a little better, and she murmured, "Thank you, sweet kitty."

Bast nuzzled her and pressed her nose to Holly's cheek.

"Sorry," Amanda apologized as she returned and eased back down on the bed.

"Where are Tante Cecile and Silvana?" Holly asked.

"They went back to their place," Amanda said. "Tante Cecile wanted to check their wards."

"Your dad?"

"Still sleeping," Amanda told her. "Or passed out. I don't know what the difference is when you're drunk." She sounded sad and bitter. Then she brightened. "Meanwhile. Geography. I found an old atlas I got in junior high. Who'd have guessed I'd ever use it?"

"Tell me about it," Holly replied, warily opening one eye.

She could see the texture of the paper as Amanda shoved the atlas under her nose. She groaned and tried to focus on the pictures. There was England.

"Do you see it? The island you saw?"

"No," Holly confessed, knowing she couldn't blame it on the image being too small. "It was right there, though," she said, pointing to where she remembered.

Amanda closed the book. "Holly, it was just a dream."

"No, it wasn't."

"Okay, suppose it wasn't. You said it was an old map. Maybe the island's not there anymore."

Holly frowned, bemused. "Are you saying it sunk or something? Like Atlantis?"

Amanda shrugged. "Could be. If it's magical."

Holly opened the book back up, her eyes barely slit open. She found the page again and stared hard at it.

"Maybe no one can see it," she said slowly. "Maybe it's simply been forgotten." She trained her acute visual strength on it, willing any hidden lands to be revealed to her.

"But . . . that makes it disappear off a map? That's unlikely."

"'Occult' means 'hidden,'" Holly reminded her.

Bast kneaded her arm, and Holly yawned as her eyelids drifted closed. She could feel sleep tugging at her; she didn't have the strength to resist any longer.

As she fell asleep, she wasn't even aware of Amanda leaving.

Morning.

And no more dreams.

Bast had wandered off, and Holly had gotten up. Now, standing in front of the bathroom mirror, squinting to avoid staring at her own pores, Holly knew what she had to do. She pulled her hair back and fastened it in place with a silver Celtic barrette and left the bathroom. She walked downstairs, rehearsing what she was going to say to Amanda.

Downstairs she found her cousin hunched over a bowl of Rice Krispies. Amanda glanced up at her.

"You slept a long time," Amanda said. "I warded my dad and checked all the house's wards." Her gaze traveled to the spot where, upstairs, her father's bedroom was located.

Holly grabbed a bowl and joined her at the table.

"I have this weird eyesight thing going," she told Amanda. "Like I'm seeing everything super close up. It's not fun."

"We'll work a spell," Amanda ventured.

"After I eat something," Holly replied. "I feel pretty nauseated."

"Have any more dreams last night?"

"No," Holly admitted. She poured in milk, stared at the bowl, and pushed it away. She knew she wouldn't be able to keep down a thing. "But I've been thinking about the one I did have."

Something in her tone must have alerted Amanda, because the other girl stopped and stared at her suspiciously. "Why do I think that I'm not going to like this?"

Holly folded her hands on the table. "Amanda, I'm going to go find Jer."

Amanda picked up her glass of orange juice and drank it down slowly. When she had drained the glass she put it down with a solid thud on the table. She locked eyes with Holly, who squinted to avoid seeing the blood vessels in her cousin's eyes.

Amanda spoke in a calm, firm voice. "Absolutely not."

"What?"

"Michael could attack again at any moment and we have to be prepared, which means we can't scatter to the four winds."

Holly took a deep breath. "I have to find him. He's

alive somewhere and I have to go to him."

Amanda did not relent. "Is that you talking or Isabeau?"

"It's me," Holly said, her temper beginning to flare. "Jer helped save us from his father before and he can help us again."

"So, this is an altruistic gesture," Amanda said sarcastically. "Nicole's already missing, and you're going to go save Michael Deveraux's son, for the good of the coven, the fight against evil."

"Absolutely." Holly nodded.

"Liar."

The word hung in the air between them. Holly felt her cheeks flame even hotter. She didn't know which made her angrier, the accusation or the fact that it was true. She stood up slowly, feeling her fingertips begin to tingle with electricity.

"I am going and I don't need your permission." She turned to go.

Amanda leaped to her feet.

"Holly, have you ever stopped to think that Michael might be deliberately doing this to divide us? We're weak without Nicole. If you go, you'll make us weaker. For all we know Jer is dead. How could he have survived the Black Fire? We both saw it burning him."

Holly slammed her fist down on the table, her desperation getting the best of her. "And whose fault is that? We were fine until you pulled me away from him!"

"Are you insane?" Amanda asked, starting to shout. "The building was falling around us; the fire was devouring everything. What was I supposed to do, leave you behind?"

Tears slid down Holly's cheeks. "We would have been fine together, the magic we share—"

"It's the magic that Isabeau and Jean share," Amanda cut her off. "It has nothing to do with the two of you. You're just the unwitting hosts. You were that night, and that's what they want again. To use you, both of you, in their own little weird twisted dance."

Holly's hand flexed and tiny sparks danced along her fingertips. "Jer and I have our own magic that has nothing to do with them."

"Really," Amanda flung at her. "Or is it just that you've got the hots for a Deveraux?"

"But I dreamed—"

"Sometimes dreams are just dreams!" Amanda yelled. "Not every dream you have means something! It's just because you freakin' want him, Holly! Get a clue!"

"Oh, yeah, then how come I have Superman's vision now?"

There was a bewildered pause from Amanda. Reluctantly she said, "Okay. That I don't know."

Holly took a deep breath. "In my dream, the woman touched my eyes and I could see everything sharper, clearer. It's like I can see everything. And I can 'see' that I'm supposed to go find him." She picked up the cereal box and thrust it into Amanda's arms. "Go over there," she ordered her cousin.

Amanda studied her for a moment. Then she strode across the kitchen. She held the box up toward Holly. "Read the ingredients for me."

Holly focused in on the box and began to read off the ingredients. "Rice, sugar, salt, high fructose corn syrup, malt flavoring."

Slowly Amanda walked back to the table and set the box of cereal back down. She looked at Holly's eyes; Holly tried hard not to squint. Then she sighed and sat back down at the table. "What the hell is malt flavoring?"

Holly shrugged. "How should I know? At least you can see I'm not lying."

Amanda clearly wanted to avoid that statement. "Regardless, Holly, I don't want you going off after Jer right now. Be patient. We'll work something out together."

"I can't be patient. Jer might not have that long," Holly said quietly.

She turned and left the room. There was no more sense in arguing.

Both had made up their minds.

"You can't leave me alone here!" Amanda yelled at her. "He'll kill us, Holly! He's just using you!"

Stricken, Holly hurried to her room, slammed the door, picked up a vase on her nightstand, and hurled it across the room.

Tommy.

Amanda grabbed her purse and stomped out the front door, answering Holly's slam and her crash— *bitch probably broke that vase. That's okay; it was ugly anyway*—and had swung her leg into the station wagon when she realized that her father was still upstairs in his stupor or whatever.

Holly can deal with him, she decided.

She had demon-dialed Tommy's number as she backed out of the driveway; it was ringing, and she flooded with relief when he picked up.

"Hello?"

"It's me," she said, "and it's all so crazy." She started to cry. "Tommy, I'm so scared and I hate this and she's talking about splitting on us and—"

"Half Caffe," he cut in. "I'd suggest you come here, but the 'rents are having some kind of Democratic fundraiser and there's no privacy. Rich knee-jerk liberals are laying their fur coats on my bed and telling me to vote for the Clean Water Bill."

Despite her mood, she smiled. Tommy Nagai had been her best friend all her life. Through thickest and thinnest, he had watched her back. She felt bad that they had started to drift a bit, now that magic took up so much of their lives.

"I know it's dicey to show in public," he continued, "but we've warded the Half Caffe pretty well, don't you think? And since Eli and Jer are both out of the picture, I'm thinking it's pretty safe. Michael's too old to know about it, unless the guys mentioned it. And my take on that family is they didn't sit around the dinner table saying, 'Would you like to hear about my exciting and fun-packed day?'"

It felt good, normal even, to listen to his banter and know that once again he was going to be a prince for her.

"I'll be there," she told him.

"Can't wait, Amanda," he replied.

Amanda.

Tommy gave his hair a brush in the men's room of the Half Caffe. He looked okay . . . for him, and if you liked Asian Americans, he was way ahead. He had excused himself from his parents' party by pointing out a window and observing to a clump of guests that since it had begun raining, there was plenty of clean water, at least for today, and his work there was done. The guests had chuckled appreciatively.

Tommy knew how to work a room.

And I think this room's clean, he thought, as he meandered back into the din that was the main hangout of Seattle's young crowd. It was a coffeehouse, decorated with oversized marble statues, murals of forests, and a balcony from which he and Amanda had spied on many of their high school friends and enemies. Their first year of college was pretty much blown, thanks to Michael Deveraux; only Tommy had managed to keep his grades going, and that had been because it was easier to do that than to deal with the parental pressure that would have resulted if they had fallen off.

He climbed the stairs to the balcony and found a table *a deux*—a section of a plaster column topped by a glass circle. The rain had made the interior gloomy, so the staff had set votive candles in little pumpkins on each table. Nearly everyone in the place had on some little bit of Halloween gear—skeleton earrings, splatter T-shirts—and Tommy felt a pang for the old days, when he and Amanda were social outcasts, Nicole was an insufferable snob, and he had wanted to shake Amanda and say to her, "I want you to be my honey, Amanda, not my best bud."

Ah, youth.

His waiter, costumed as Count Dracula, stalked him until he ordered stuff he knew Amanda would like: chai tea latte and a cinnamon roll. Then the waiter was happy, plopped down a couple of waters, and left Tommy to wait for Amanda.

And there she is.

She rushed in, looking nervous, closing up her umbrella as she shook an errant raindrop or two from her curly, light brown hair. She hadn't been cutting it as much—no time, when warlocks are trying to kill you—and he liked the softness around her face.

She saw him, waved, and came up the stairs. They hugged, because they always did, but this time Tommy held her for a few beats longer.

She started sniffling against his shoulder. Alarmed, he drew away, then realized she wanted him to stay put; he put his arms around her, soothed her, saying, "Shh, shh, I bought you a roll."

She giggled softly and went to her chair.

He was sorry about that, but he took his own and raised his brows, ready to listen.

"She wants to split. She had this dream. Jer's on an

island and she wants to go to him," Amanda said in a rush.

"An island," he repeated.

She rolled her eyes. "In England, or somewhere near England."

"Ah." He folded his arms. "Because there are so few there. Just the Orkneys, and, oh, tiny Britain itself, and—"

"And we've got warlocks trying to kill us and all she can think about is her one true love, who is also a warlock."

"Movies these days," he said smoothly, as the waiter brought over the tea chai latte's and the roll.

"Yeah," she replied, getting it.

They waited while their things were placed on the table. Then Amanda sat back in her chair and sighed heavily.

"This dream," he ventured.

"He's locked up. Or something. I don't know. She can't leave us here by ourselves. We'll be massacred."

He agreed, but he didn't say anything. He just let her talk.

"It's not fair, it's not right, and I think we should tell her she can't go. She's our High Priestess, for god's sake!"

"In the same movie," he continued, as the waiter

came by again to refill their water glasses.

To his surprise, Amanda guffawed. She pounced on his left hand, which was lying innocently on the table, and said, "Oh, Tommy, I just love you!"

His heart skipped a beat. *Oh, if only you did,* he told her silently. *Amanda, a truer heart has never pumped oxygenated blood cells. . . .*

He picked up his cup and said, "We should hold a circle. Talk to her. You're right; she can't act as if she's not part of a greater whole. We're already all pissed off at Nicole."

She released his hand and he was very sorry about that. But her eyes had a new shiny quality to them, as if she were looking at him a little differently, and he dared hope . . .

. . . as he had been hoping for over ten years . . .

"You're right. We should hold a circle. Oh, Tommy, what would I do without you?" she chirruped.

He smiled gently at her. "Let's don't find out."

Her lips bowed upward; her cheeks got rosy, and yes, there was definitely something new in her eyes.

"Let's don't," she agreed.

Michael: Seattle, October

It was Samhain—Halloween—and upstairs the doorbell kept ringing. Michael knew the trick-or-treaters were confused and disappointed; the Deveraux house was usually one of the best places to go. Intent upon maintaining good ties with the community, his treats were always very lavish.

This year, he had better things to do on the night of one of Coventry's major sabbats.

Now in the black heart of his home—the chamber of spells—he had donned his special Samhain robe, decorated with red leering pumpkins, green leaves, and blood droplets and brought out special ritual arcane: green-black candles in which swirled human blood; a ritual bowl cut from the skull of a witch hanged at Salem; even a special athame, presented to him by his father the first time he had raised one of the dead.

Observing the preparations, the imp sat and stared, as imps will—impishly—at Michael. Michael took a deep breath, forcing himself to be calm and centered before the ritual. Excitement was rippling through him though. Through throwing the runes and reading the entrails of several small sacrifices, he had verified the truth of the curse of the Cahors. Their loved ones usually died by drowning.

He had a wonderful new way to strike out at the Cahors.

Chanting in Latin, he reached into a tank of water and pulled a baby shark out by the tail. He held the gasping creature above the altar and raised his knife in his other hand. "Oh, horned god, accept this my sacrifice. Raise up all the demons and creatures of the sea that they might aid me in destroying the Cahors family."

He stabbed the squirming shark and let its blood drip onto some dried coriander and bitter root on the altar. When the creature at last stopped squirming he dropped the body upon the altar as well. He picked up a candle and set the herbs on fire; in moments the body of the shark ignited and began to burn.

Michael leaned forward to breathe in the smoke. The stench was terrible, but the feeling of power was almost overwhelming. He closed his eyes. "Let the creatures of the sea hear my voice and obey me. Kill the witches. Kill every last Cahors.

"Let all the demons harken to my cry. Today the Cahors witches must die. *Emergo, volito, perficio meum nutum!*"

In the smoke above the altar, images slowly appeared, snapping into clarity . . . and into reality. Off the coast, sharks cast back and forth as though catching a scent of blood in the water. They worked themselves into a frenzy as they moved closer and closer toward the shore.

Farther out to sea the ocean began to boil. Dead

fish bobbed and floated to the surface, cooked completely through in an instant. The waters roiled, and slowly from the depths of the ocean something stirred, awakening.

It groped its way from its watery grave, hungry, searching. Blind from having lived so long in the blackness at the bottom of the ocean, it could still sense movement near it. Every living thing fled before it in terror. It opened its mouth to expose hideous teeth, jagged and each nearly a foot long.

Spiny scales covered its eel-like head as it cast this way and that searching for its prey. Slowly its serpent body unfurled itself and its powerful legs began to thrash. Long toes with wicked nails slashed through the water as it made its way to the surface, killing everything in its path.

Only the water sprites who sailed through the water like silent ghosts did not run from it. Instead they laughed soundlessly and spiraled around it.

"On this Halloween night, a killer whale has tipped over a small fishing boat. Witnesses who were on a nearby vessel saw the beast ram into the boat hard enough to flip it. The two men inside the boat disappeared and it is not known whether they drowned or were killed. In other news . . ."

Holly turned off the car radio.

She pulled up to the cliff from where she liked to stare out at the ocean and stopped the car. She got out, still squinting. Driving had been a trick with the enhanced vision, but she thought it was maybe starting to fade.

That would be a distinct relief.

She sighed as she strode to the edge of the cliff and looked out at the waves. Something wasn't right. There was a dark spot not that far from shore; she frowned and strained her superpower eyes, trying to see what it was. A fin broke the surface of the water on the edge of the spot; then another and another until she saw ten of them: sharks.

They were diving in and out of the spot; with a shudder Holly realized that it must be blood. They had killed something, and from the looks of it, it was large. She watched the ocean predators circling and diving, and though she felt afraid and somewhat repulsed, she couldn't force herself to look away.

At last the activity began to die down and the sharks turned in a pack and begin swimming up the coast. The spot remained behind, not breaking up on the water, like a shadow.

Her cell phone rang and she jumped. Her hand was shaking slightly as she pulled the phone from her purse.

"Yeah?"

It was Amanda. Holly half-listened to her cousin as she watched the fins slowly disappear in the distance. The coven was meeting to discuss her desire to rescue Jer.

"All right," she said coolly. She felt defensive. *They have no right to keep me from going if that's what I have to do.*

"We're going to meet on the Port Townsend ferry," Amanda continued. Port Townsend was a beautiful enclave of old Victorian homes on an island across the bay.

"Ferry?" Holly asked, the word piercing through the thoughts in her head. "But, Amanda . . ."

"Tante Cecile has said protection spells. She also says it's the only place we can discuss this privately. *He* has spies everywhere."

"But—"

"Just do it, Holly," Amanda snapped.

Amanda hung up.

"It's not safe," Holly murmured to the dial tone. "I know it's not safe."

As Holly turned and walked back to her car, Michael stared into his scrying stone and smiled.

Seated beside him in Michael's chamber of spells, the imp's grin broadened. He opened his mouth and spoke in a perfect imitation of Amanda's voice, "'Just do it, Holly.'"

Michael laughed. "Now do Tante Cecile."

"'You'll be safest on the ferry, Amanda,'" he mimicked.

"That's great. That's perfect." He patted the creature on its back.

Part Two
Full

☾

"When the moon in the sky is round and bright
Evil comes out to play that night
Witches cavort and mad men rave
And creatures reach out from beyond the grave."

——Druid Prophecy

FIVE

QUIET MOON

☾

Green man hear us as we plead
Grant us the power that we need
In the darkness we crouch and wait
Help us as we hone our hate

Goddess help us in our quest
Keep our enemies from rest
In the stillness let them hear
Their own hearts pound loud in fear

The Cathers/Anderson Coven: Seattle, October

Kari frowned as she glanced at her watch. She was leaving her apartment, joining the throngs of Halloween celebrants as she walked toward the secured parking lot where she kept her car.

She was running late to catch the ferry for the Circle meeting. She and Circle Lady had been engrossed in an e-mail conversation that she had been loathe to break. The two had spent less time contacting each other as

Kari became more involved with the coven. It was safer that way, but she missed the conversations with the other woman, so it had been a nice surprise when Circle Lady had IMed her about an hour ago and said, "How are you?"

At least, I think she's a woman. Problem with the Internet is you never can tell.

Kari had spent time pouring out her frustrations about Jer and Holly to Circle Lady—boy-girl stuff, like how come "Warlock" had basically dumped her and what could she do about it? Of course she hadn't mentioned anything about magic, battles, blood feuds, possession, or Black Fire. In fact, she'd managed to leave magic out of the conversation almost entirely.

Circle Lady had asked a few questions about Warlock—how he was, etcetera—and Kari had shot back, "Who knows?"

Which was true.

She was at the lot; the attendant, dressed in devil red, a pair of short horns sticking out of his dark hair, grinned at her as he unlocked the gate.

"You goin' to a party?" he asked conversationally.

"Yes," she replied, distracted. "A party. Uh-huh."

"No costume," he chided.

"I'm going as a witch."

He shook his head. "You need a broom. Pointy hat."

She glanced uneasily at the sky, looking for falcons, glancing around for burning bushes, not loving any of this. She remembered the conversations she had used to have with Jer back when she was stupid and naive, had done everything she could to get him interested in her so he would show some magic to her. She had begged him to let her help him with his rituals. It had all been so exciting back then, dark and a little dangerous.

Well, now it's a lot dangerous, and I'm not sure how long I can take this. Nicole had the right idea bailing like she did. If it wasn't for school I'd be out of here in a minute.

That wasn't entirely true.

Okay, and if I knew Jer was safe, the dork. Even if he's hot on Holly, I still care about him.

She drove to the ferry landing, parked, figured out which ferry to take, and noticed with a mixture of relief and apprehension that it hadn't left yet.

I wouldn't mind missing this meeting. Sparks are gonna fly, if I know Holly. And I am not loving meeting on a ferry in the middle of Elliott Bay. We might as well hold signs over our heads for Michael to read: DEAD MEAT.

She hesitated for only a moment before climbing out of her car. After all, there was safety in numbers, and the way things had been lately, she could use a little safety.

★ ★ ★

The ferries of Washington State were sleek and modern vessels replete with nice lounges and snack bars. As the costumed crowd swarmed onto the Port Townsend ferry, Holly got herself a Diet Coke and found a large table that would accommodate the entire coven, if they squished in. She wondered if Kialish's father would show. He was a friend of the coven but not a member. Maybe he would feel that he had no right to interfere.

She sipped her soda, waiting nervously, distractedly admiring some of the costumes—lots of fairies, lots of guys with pretend axes in their chests—wondering what was going to happen. She pressed her fingers to her temples; she'd have to ask Amanda for some aspirin when she showed up. The last of the supervision seemed to have gone, but it had left a nasty headache. It didn't help that she couldn't figure out why on earth Tante Cecile had insisted they meet on water.

Last call was sounded and the ferry began to cast off from the dock. It was after dark, and the glittering lights of the Emerald City played out in the side windows; ahead, the water was dark and deep.

There was still no sign of anyone else, and she began to worry.

Did something happen to them?

She wasn't certain whether she should go in search of them or stay put; she decided to stay where she was.

The engines picked up speed and the ferry moved into the waters, leaving behind the city.

Still she waited. Half an hour dragged by.

Then she finally saw Eddie, who turned and gestured to someone behind him. Kari and Amanda caught up to him, Kari glaring at her; the three trooped toward her, and Kari demanded, "Where have you been?"

"What do you mean?" Holly frowned. "I've been here. Isn't this where we planned to meet?" It seemed the logical location.

"You weren't here," Amanda chimed in, also looking peeved.

"I was too." Holly felt her temper rise. "You must have missed me." Then she looked past the three of them. "Where's everyone else?"

"We don't know," Eddie said, looking unhappy. "We figured they were with you."

"Something's up," Holly said. "Meeting out here is crazy."

"Tante Cecile said it was the best place," Amanda said. "She called me and said so."

"Well, where is she?" Holly asked.

"Look," Eddie cut in. "Whatever's going on, I

don't like it. And I for sure don't like the idea of you splitting on us to go on your big quest to 'save' Jeraud Deveraux. You're our leader. You can't abandon us the way Nicole did."

Holly took a deep breath. "I thought about that."

Eddie visibly relaxed, his sharp features softening. "Oh?"

Kari, however, frowned and said, "Holly, if you sense that he's alive and you don't do something about it—"

"I'm going to do something about it," she cut in, her voice rising. "I'm handing leadership of the coven over to Amanda."

"Fine," Amanda bit off. "I'm leader." She glared at Holly. "You can't go."

"You have to be leader." Eddie balled his fists in anger. "You were chosen to be the leader. You carry the power."

It was Holly's turn to raise her voice. "Don't tell me what to do, Eddie. Your coven couldn't protect him. What makes you think ours can? The vision got sent to *me*. By my ancestor. To save him."

"Because she's in love with Jean!" Amanda exploded. "She doesn't give a rat's ass about what's happening to us with Michael. She's obsessed with her dead lover, and they can be together through Jer and you. She was as ruthless in her day as any Deveraux, and she doesn't care who dies trying to save her little channeling partner."

"I . . . I . . ." Holly faltered. *I love him. But Amanda has a point. Is that any reason to abandon these guys?*

"I forbid you to go," Amanda announced, drawing herself up imperiously. "And I will do everything in my power, magically and otherwise, to keep you from going."

As if on cue, the floor began to shake. The walls rattled; some guys at the next table over frowned and said to Holly's group, "Wow, tough takeoff. We're from Montana. Do they always do that?"

"No," Holly said, glancing at Amanda. "And they don't take off, exactly."

The vessel shuddered again. Voices began to rise. A man got to his feet and said over his shoulder, "I'm going to go see what's going on."

"Something's wrong," Holly said. She stood.

The others followed.

As they made their way out of the snack area and past the rows of theater-style chairs, the enormous report of an explosion rocked Holly and sent her sprawling. Parts of the ceiling fell loose; a window buckled; the boat began to list.

Claxons blared an alarm. A man's voice interrupted the elevator music that had been playing and said,

"Ladies and gentlemen, please stay calm. Please proceed to a designated life jacket area, where you will receive a life jacket from one of our easily identifiable crew members. Please stay completely calm. There is no reason for panic."

"Bite me!" Eddie shouted. "There's plenty of reason!"

Scrambling out of the middle of the walkway toward the wall, then thinking better of it because of the exploding windows, Holly closed her eyes and invoked protection; Amanda joined in, and then Kari and Eddie. They ran, joining hands; as one, without discussion, they went outside.

"Are there life jackets out here?" an anxious woman wearing a cheery Halloween sweater yelled in Holly's face. When Holly didn't respond quickly enough, the woman darted past her to another passenger, glomming on to him and shouting, "I need a life jacket!"

The ferry was lurching forward awkwardly like a giant child's pull toy on a string. It was also listing heavily to the right. Passengers were fleeing out the doors, jostling the four; screams rose in the night as the shriek of grinding metal rose higher and higher.

Then a strange, alien wailing filled the air, joining with the claxons in a terrible cacophony. The wailing was coming off the side of the ship; Holly burst through the massing throngs and fought her way to the railing.

"Oh, my God," she breathed, looking down into the water.

Shrouded in darkness, occasionally illuminated by the lights of the ferry, it was a nightmare, a creature composed of huge taloned claws, tentacles, a clawed beak, and eyes that glared balefully up at her. In its eyes—each as large as a car tire, each a bloodshot circle of blackness—gleamed not precisely intelligence, but an evil intention, a hunger, a glee. It blinked when it saw Holly.

It knows me.

Birds wheeled overhead, shrieking and screaming as they dive-bombed at Holly. She saw that they were falcons, blue-black and aggressive, several times nearly hitting her as she ducked.

Then creatures emerged from the dark water on either side of the monster; they were of vaguely human shape, but covered with scales, their fingers hooked. As Holly watched, they hammered their hooks into the side of the ferry and climbed their way up the hull, very fast, very close.

The ship listed again, harder.

Eddie came up beside her and grabbed her arm. "I

think it's going to sink," he shouted.

She pointed. "Look."

As its minions hoisted themselves nearly to the top of the rail, the monster rose from the waters, hefting itself up on some giant stalk or pair of legs—God knew what—and its tentacles whipped in Holly and Eddie's direction.

Eddie grabbed her, throwing his arms around her and pulling her away from the side.

The ferry canted again. Passengers lost their footing and slid toward the wheelhouse containing the snack bar and the rows of chairs. Holly and Eddie were swept up by the momentum, and together they slammed hard against the bulkhead.

Amanda was on the ground with a huge gash in her forehead. Kari was bending over her, shouting to Holly, "Do something!"

"Amanda, are you okay?" Holly cried. She put her hand on her cousin's head and murmured, "Heal her, my Goddess."

Amanda looked up at her, blood gushing from the wound. "The Goddess isn't the one who put it there, Holly."

"Michael Deveraux!" Kari shouted to the falcons swarming above them. "I'm going to kill you myself!"

I knew this meeting was wrong. I knew it! Holly

thought, fury mingling with fear. *I should have said something, should have refused to come.*

Water rushed through the doors of the snack bar, swirling up to their ankles, then their knees. Holly realized that the opposite side of the vessel was underwater, and she said to the four, "Grab hands. Hold on tight."

With a grunt, she forced Amanda to her feet and half-walked, half-dragged her to a crew member who stood beside an unlocked bin of life jackets. People were fighting one another for them, grabbing at the orange vests as the beleaguered man tried to pass them out. Holly realized their chances of getting some were next to nothing.

She said, "Keep holding on to one another. We're strongest that way. Concentrate. Keep your eyes open and look into one another's eyes. We're going to see ourselves living through this. We're going to envision survival, embody survival."

Kari's glance ticked to the left, and she let out a terrible scream.

One of the creature's tentacles was whipsawing the crowd. As Holly watched in horror, a man's head was sliced cleanly off his body. Another's arm was severed; blood gushed from his shoulder socket, mingling with the frigid, rising water.

Holly looked left, right; she had no idea what to do. Other people were scrambling onto the side of the wheelhouse, tilted at a frightening angle.

The birds dove at them, screaming.

"Oh, my God. Oh, my God," Amanda panted.

"Stare into my eyes. See yourself surviving," Holly ordered her. "See it."

"I can't. I can't. I can't," Amanda gasped. "Holly, oh, my God . . ."

"You will survive." Holly willed her to feel it, know it.

Then the waters rushed around them, buoying them away like tiny woodchips; they sailed end over end; Holly shut her eyes tight and held on as tightly as she could to Amanda's hand . . . to Amanda's hand . . . to Amanda's hand . . .

She held on for dear life, literally, as they plunged into the black, icy waters; she held on as tightly as she could and tried to kick toward the surface. There were people all around her, grasping, kicking, punching in their terror. She couldn't see a thing, only blackness.

Isabeau, she thought, shifting from praying to the Goddess to begging her ancestress for help. *Please, save us.*

Then miraculously, her head broke the surface. Amanda's too; she saw it by the light of the ferry, which was sinking.

Holly saw what was happening, but it didn't register.

"We need to conjure," she said to her cousin. "We need to focus."

Amanda was sobbing hysterically. Holly gave up, looked around for the others.

"Eddie? Kari?"

"Here," Eddie announced. "I don't know where she is. I can't find her."

"We have to conjure," she repeated to him.

"Kialish," he moaned. "Kialish, I'm gonna die without saying good-bye to him."

"Don't be stupid. We're not going to die."

"It's your curse, Holly. You're cursing us to die."

"You're not going to die," she repeated.

Fresh screams erupted from the other water-bound passengers, announcing a new horror. Holly looked over her shoulder, and that was when she lost it too.

The humanoid creatures were swimming through the throng, raising their talons and chopping randomly into people as they went. Their talons were knife-sharp; the wounds were deep. Most of their victims stopped screaming as soon as they made contact.

And trailing in their wake was the monster.

Holly tried to fight down her own panic, moving down inside herself, finding a place, a center. The rest of her being panicked around it; yet she said, "I abjure thee, I repulse thee, minion of evil. Get thee hence!"

Her words had no effect on it. It rose to a great height as if it were naturally buoyant; she saw its quivering, filthy mass, the tentacles everywhere, the mess that was its head. In its beak it carried a young woman who very quickly stopped struggling and hung limp in its grasp. It chomped her in two; her torso and head hit the water. It tossed away the other half and lumbered ahead, toward Holly.

Eddie swam in front of her, shouting, "Get me! Get me, you bastard!"

"Eddie, no!" It was an unnecessary gesture; if that thing wanted to kill her, it would. She waved at Eddie to stop, and Amanda's grip slackened and went limp.

Amanda let go of Holly's hand, and her head slipped below the surface.

"Amanda!" Holly shouted, and dove underwater to find her.

It was pitch black and crowded, but a faint blue glow guided Holly directly downward. She swam as hard as she could, chasing the glow.

Down she spiraled, and farther down; her lungs were about to explode. She reached the glow, stretched out a hand . . . and it faded and winked out.

No! Holly thought, lunging forward, feeling the

water. Other bodies bumped into her, pieces of sea-weed, and what she hoped were fish.

But of her cousin there was no sign.

Unable to stay below the surface any longer, she rose, sucking in air as she broke the surface.

As if by . . . *magic,* a life ring bobbed beside her. She grabbed it.

And then she panicked at what she saw.

The water was thick with blood, and one of the minion-creatures slashed at her; it was less than a foot away. Its immense companion rushed toward her—

—*game over, I'm dead*—

"Holly," Eddie moaned.

He floated about three feet away to her left. She began to lunge for him . . . until she realized that Amanda had resurfaced, facedown, and bobbed on the waves about five feet away in the opposite direction.

The creatures were bearing down.

"Holly," Eddie said again. He looked at her, reached a hand for her. "I'm hurt."

There was no more time to think, to choose; with a choked sob, Holly pushed the life ring toward Amanda, looped her arm around it and yanked her head out of the water so that her chin was propped up, and began to kick as hard as she could.

She invoked protection spell after protection spell,

begging, pleading with the Goddess and with Isabeau to save her. A talon swiped at her, catching the edge of her heel, and she would have screamed if she could have remembered how. . . .

Then gunfire erupted over her head, someone shooting from in front of her at the monsters. Someone shouting, "Here!"

And Holly managed to look up as she fought for her own life, and for Amanda's, swimming in her icy, sodden clothes; swimming despite the fact that she had no strength left.

A Coast Guard cutter had roared up, followed by another, and another; there was a flotilla of them, and they were shooting at the monsters. Then one of them was throwing her another life ring, but her hands were too numb to catch it. She croaked in frustration—she could no longer speak—and then began to whimper, blinded by panic.

She forced herself to find her calm center again. *I am a Cathers witch,* she thought.

She stared down at her hands, willing them to grab the life ring. Somehow she managed to position Amanda's cold, limp body onto the ring. She gave the line a tug.

"Holly!" Eddie screamed.

She turned to go back to him, but at that moment,

Amanda slipped off the life ring and began to go under. Holly grabbed her, holding on to the ring.

The Coast Guard officer began to reel them in. If she let go of Amanda, her cousin would slide back into the water.

"Holly!" She could hear the terror in Eddie's voice. "Holly, help!"

She turned around; Amanda shifted on the flotation device and she grabbed hold of her.

She couldn't see Eddie anywhere. The water was a swarm of monsters, dying people, and the leviathan that even now moved toward her.

The Coast Guardsman reeled her in; she sobbed as she was pulled onto the deck, as they put a blanket around her shoulders, and as a medic on board gave her something to calm her down.

She saw that Kari had been rescued as well, and tried to be grateful for that.

But she would not be soothed.

Goddess, protect him, she supplicated.

But she knew in the depths of her soul that Eddie was dead.

France, 13th Century

Catherine was dying. Whether through poison or magic or simple bad luck, she could not tell. But she was dying; there was no doubt.

The Deveraux had not won; but then, neither had she. Both covens had lost untold celebrants in the massacre of Deveraux Castle on Beltane, and the resultant reprisals that went on even now, six years later.

She called her new protégé, Marie, to her bedside. The young girl was sixteen and a very good witch. Catherine had imbued her with magical powers, and the girl had understood her role in Coventry: At all costs, the Cahors line must be perpetuated.

Pandion the lady hawk sat on the ornate headboard of Catherine's bed of state. She had slept alone in it for three years, since the death of her second husband, although she had entertained more lovers in it than she could count. They, however, were not allowed to sleep the night there.

But all that was over, and she would soon be dust.

"So many of us are ashes now," she said to the beautiful young girl. Curls tumbled down Marie's back; she was very slender, and her eyes were enormous. She put Catherine in mind of Isabeau, her only child, her dear child.

"To protect you and our coven, I am sending you away," she told the girl. "To England. There are followers of the Circle there who will help you; you will be looked after." She sighed. "I abandoned Jeannette, but I will not abandon you."

"Oui, madame," the girl said feelingly. Her eyes brimmed with tears. "I shall do as you command, in all things, always."

"There's a good girl," Catherine murmured. Then her breath snaked out of her body, and she was dead.

Marie devoutly bowed her head and prayed to the Goddess to lead her through fields of lilies.

"And let her find Isabeau, whom she always loved," she finished.

Then she clapped her hands. Servants appeared instantly, gasping aloud at the sight of their *grande dame,* dead in her bed.

"She shall be burned and put in the garden," Marie informed them.

And I shall not be there to witness it.

I am bound for England, as my mistress wished.

Eli Deveraux: London, Samhain

The innocent called it Halloween.

But in Coventry new marriages were made, old feuds forgotten . . . and sacrifices made.

Eli Deveraux looked up with satisfaction from the

grisly remains of a young woman whose still-beating heart he held in his fist. Her thick, red blood ran down his arm and dripped onto the stone floor of the ancient chamber where he wrought his magic.

"This, my brother's heart," he intoned, showing the heart to the statue of the horned god, who crouched on the altar. "Help me kill him, Great God Pan. Send my familiar to do my work."

There was a great flapping of wings; then the immortal falcon, Fantasme, scowled at Eli and cocked his head. Eli held out the heart, and the bird glided toward it. Fantasme was not a stranger to human sacrifice.

Another young woman, this one very much alive, entered the private chamber and inclined her head. She was dressed in a gossamer robe, and she was here to be his Lady to the Lord, so that he could perform some very high-level magics. He had recruited her to help him during a ritual with Sir William in attendance; Eli was certain she had agreed not because she wanted to, but because she was afraid to refuse him.

"Undress," he said coldly. He wasn't sure why he disliked her now, but he did. He had looked forward to their coupling, which would produce the potent magical energy he required.

I'm just in a bad mood, he told himself. *Learning that*

Jer is alive has put me in a funk. I thought I was rid of him, and now . . . he's like a bad penny.

At least he's in terrible pain and hideously scarred.

Proving that there is a God.

The girl stood undressed. In a voice dripping with hostility, Eli said, "Get ready."

She lay on the altar, waiting for him.

Why did she say yes? he wondered. *Is it some kind of trap?*

And then it didn't matter as he joined her on the altar; he knew then that she had consented because he did something for her. A lot of women liked Eli Deveraux, liked his aura of menace, all that power . . .

That cheered him up a little.

Blue magic began to churn in the room, sweeping over the altar, shining along Eli's athame and the girl's robe. The room began to dance with it. The gray statue's eyes glowed blue; its mouth turned up in a smile.

When it was done, Eli felt stronger, more concentrated, and more focused. Pulling on a green robe decorated with red clusters of holly berries, he picked up the heart again and said, "My lord, I offer this to you, if you will only kill my brother."

The stone jaw of the statue dropped open; the neck extended forward, the eyes rolled downward. In strange, lockstep motions, the statue plucked up the heart, and silently devoured it.

The girl watched in startled fascination.

I'll take that as a yes, Eli thought. He was overjoyed.

My God is going to kill my brother.

So it's a happy Halloween after all.

SIX

HUNGER MOON

☾

Cahors witches best beware
As we take to the air
We will kill them where they stand
Everywhere throughout the land

Now we chew upon each bone
Granted us by the Crone
We shall feast with next moon rise
On our victim as he slowly dies

Nicole: Spain, All Hallow's Eve

They had been in the safe house for a week. This particular night, Nicole was asleep as soon as her head hit the pillow. When a hand on her shoulder shook her gently awake, it was dark. Philippe stood beside her, smiling faintly. "Come on. Time to get up."

"What time is it?" she asked.

"Nearly midnight."

"The witching hour?" She smiled.

He laughed low. "You could say that."

He was again dressed in his cloak, but the hood was folded back behind his head. He held out a cloak to her as she sat up. "You can put this on."

She grimaced. "What I'd really like are some clean clothes."

He gestured to the foot of her bed where she saw a shirt and a folded up pair of jeans. "There is a young lady at the villa who is about the same size as you. She donated some clothing."

"Was this your idea?" she asked, surprised.

"Actually it was José Luís's," he conceded. "Come, hurry, *ma belle*. Everyone else is outside; come out when you're dressed."

"*Merci*, Philippe."

Nicole sat up as soon as he left. She spied a water pitcher and a basin on a small table and gratefully discovered that the pitcher had been freshly filled. She peeled off her shirt and splashed some water over her face and shoulders.

She put on the clothes and was pleased to find that they were only a little loose. She ran her fingers through her hair and winced as she tried to pull out the tangles. She must look a fright. *If Amanda could see me now, she wouldn't believe it.* It was a far cry from her days as a beauty queen.

She grimaced as she put on the cloak. The material was thick and course. She lifted the hood up over her head to test the feel. She shuddered slightly as the material engulfed her. Quickly she folded the hood back.

She took a deep breath and opened the door. Outside the five warlocks stood in a loose cluster looking like ghosts in the darkness. As one they turned toward her, the gentle murmur of conversation ceased. She stepped among them, her heart beginning to pound. Dressed as they were it was impossible not to feel a sense of connection, of belonging.

Someone had brought the car up close, and they all piled in except for Armand. As Philippe started the engine, Nicole gestured to the lone figure outside.

"Isn't he coming with us?"

Philippe shook his head. "He will rejoin us soon. For now he has to wipe out the memory of us from this place."

At her look of slight confusion, Alonzo explained, "Have you ever been someplace where you could feel the history, as though the walls were speaking to you?"

She nodded slowly. "I felt that once. My family went to Washington, D.C., to see some old friends. They took us to see the Ford Theatre where President Lincoln was shot. I felt as though if I closed my eyes I could see it all happening. Is that what you mean?"

"*Sí.* People and events leave their imprint upon places. The walls of a building, for instance, record on a psychic level the events that happen within them. It is just like a path in a forest where animals and people leave footprints. The average person never sees these marks, but to an experienced tracker they are clear and reveal much about the creatures that left them.

"In the same way the average person never senses the psychic imprints left on places unless those imprints are unusually strong, and then they often claim that the place has history or is haunted. To a trained tracker, though—"

"The psychic imprints we leave behind are as easily read as tracks on a trail," Nicole finished.

"Yes. Armand is staying behind to cover the traces of our passage, much as though he were scraping a branch along the ground and obliterating footprints."

Nicole shivered. "If he weren't, could someone really find us that way?"

"I could," Pablo answered quietly.

Nicole twisted in the front seat so she could look back at the boy. His eyes shone in the darkness.

"That you could," Philippe affirmed. "So, Armand will catch up with us when he's finished."

"Armand is good at blocking. I can't read him," Pablo said.

She continued to stare at the boy as she thought, *Unlike me?*

He smiled slowly and he looked like a wolf baring its teeth.

Nicole turned back around. She would have to have a talk with Armand later.

They drove in what seemed a winding and circuitous fashion for two hours, skirting at least one village. They pulled off the road and drove for a few more miles. When they finally stopped it was in a large flat field. There were no structures of any kind in view.

"We have several hours yet before dawn. We will wait here for Armand, and when he joins us we will have the ceremony," José Luís announced.

From the trunk of the car the others pulled out firewood and several packets of what looked like herbs. As they began laying the wood out in preparation for a fire, Nicole turned to Philippe.

"Aren't you afraid someone will see the fire?"

He shook his head. "They will enchant it so that only we and Armand can see it. It will help guide him to us. Come, while they are working we will talk."

He led her a little ways away so that they could still see the rest of the coven but they could not be overheard. He sat and motioned for her to do likewise.

Once she was seated facing him he asked, "Who is chasing you, Nicole?"

"I don't know," she stammered, feeling her heart begin to race.

He nodded gravely and took both her hands in his. "Whoever it is is very powerful. Nicole, I fear for you. We must take extra care."

Nicole felt herself crumble. She was tired of all this; she left Seattle to get away from the witchcraft and the danger. At least she wasn't alone.

"I'm glad you found me." She sobbed.

He shrugged and reddened slightly. "I have a confession: Our meeting was no accident. We have been searching for you, Nicole of the Cahors, since we heard that you were in Spain."

She bristled, anxious that they had "heard" of her, hurt that he hadn't told her before. "It's Anderson," she replied icily, not yet sure how she was going to respond to the other.

"Maybe to them," he gestured wide, indicating the world with a sweep of his arm. "But here, with us, and here," he tapped her chest over her heart, "you are Cahors. Yours is an old family, and there is pride to be taken in that."

"My ancestors were murderers and assassins. No pride there."

"Not all," he answered gently. "Some Cahors witches were allied with the covens of the Light and they did much good. Others chose to ally themselves with all the forces of Darkness. And only you, Nicole, can say which side you shall ally yourself with."

She smiled bitterly. "I would be lying if I denied that I was drawn to the dark." She thought of Eli and the excitement she had felt when she was with him. She thought of the things they had done together, how she had let him touch her, and she was filled with mixed emotions. Mainly she felt remorse but there was a small part of her that was defiant, that knew that even with the knowledge she had now, she might not change a thing if given the choice. That was the part that frightened her.

Her scalp began to tingle, and she looked away from him. She glanced toward the others and was unnerved to find Pablo staring straight at her. His eyes bore into hers. Did he know what she was thinking? She fervently hoped not and tried to wipe her earlier thoughts from her mind. He shook his head slowly, whether in disapproval or defeat she did not know. At last he turned away and she felt herself sag with relief.

"Pablito sometimes uses his gifts when he ought not. Unfortunately, discretion is one of those things that only time teaches young men," Philippe observed, having watched the exchange.

Nicole looked back at him guiltily. "Maybe he's right to keep an eye on me."

He smiled. "Time will tell the truth of that. But for now, come. They are ready for the ceremony."

He stood and extended his hand. She took it and he helped pull her to her feet. Together they walked back to the fire.

"What sort of ceremony is it?"

"A seeking ceremony. We are asking for visions of the future."

"So, what, I get to ask to see my future husband?" she joked.

He gave her an appraising look. "Perhaps you will, but it is not for me to say. No one can choose what they are shown."

As they reached the fire, Nicole noticed that Armand had rejoined them. He nodded at her briefly.

"Now that we are together, we shall begin," José Luís announced.

They all seated themselves around the fire. The smoke drifting upward carried the scent of burning wood mixed with something else that was much sweeter. Nicole wrinkled her nose, not sure whether the smell was a pleasing one.

They joined hands, and for one wild moment

Nicole thought they were all going to start singing "Kumbayah." She closed her eyes, willing herself to relax, and took a few deep breaths. The sweet smell wasn't that unpleasant, she decided. It was actually kind of nice.

"We are gathered here to invoke the power of Seeing. We ask for clarity about the path that we are on, where it is leading, and what we must do to uphold the Light. Show us what we must see," Philippe finished.

"Grant us eyes that we might see," Armand added.

"Grant us wisdom to know what we must do," Alonzo said.

"Grant us courage that we might act," Pablo said.

"Grant us strength that we might prevail," José Luís concluded.

On either side of her, José Luís and Alonzo released her hands. Nicole opened her eyes and watched as Alonzo picked up a long, crooked white stick that had been sitting on top of the fire. She gasped as she heard the sizzling wood burning his palm. He held it close to his chest and bent his head over it, eyes squeezed tightly shut.

Nicole watched as the muscle that ran along the left side of his jaw twitched. At last he looked up and his eyes shone brightly. "I see a great evil reaching across Europe, its darkness sweeps everything away before it."

He passed the stick to Armand and picked up a strip of cloth soaking in a bowl of liquid. Gingerly he wrapped it around his burned hand.

Armand bowed his head over the stick reverently. His entire body began to shake. Finally he looked up. "I see myself standing between the Darkness and the Light. We are fighting the Darkness and we are not alone. Others are with us, but there is a great price to be paid."

He passed the stick wordlessly to Philippe and then took a towel from the bowl handed to him by Alonzo and wrapped his hand. Philippe bowed over the stick for only a moment before looking back up. Tears were shining in his eyes.

"I see myself taking up a great burden and lifting it from the shoulders of another. The burden ages me."

He passed the stick to Pablo and took a cloth. The young guy bent over the stick for several minutes quietly before he at last looked up.

"I see an island that has been hidden for centuries. There is a man in chains. A woman watches over him; she has always watched over him. She is afraid. Someone else is on the island, and he frightens her."

José Luís took the stick from Pablo and held it tightly. Nicole could smell his flesh burning as she watched the tendons in his fingers flexing.

At last he looked up. His voice was eerily calm as he spoke. "I see my death."

Shocked, Nicole stared at the stick as he offered it to her. She didn't want to take it, didn't want to be burned, and she certainly didn't want to see anything. Still, she reached out her hand and clasped the stick. Her flesh burned and she knew it, but she could feel nothing. She held the stick in front of her.

She saw Eli's face floating before her, laughing, taunting. It faded and another face was there above her. The features were cruel and twisted beneath a mane of blond hair. She screamed and tossed the stick from her.

Alonzo caught the stick in midair and after saying a few words over it, set it gently down. José Luís began wrapping her burned hand in the soothing cloth. "What did you see?" he pressed.

She looked up at him, gasping for air. She had never seen that face before in her life, and yet now she gasped, clawing for breath as if her head was still under the water in the bathtub at the safe house, "I saw . . . I saw . . . *my husband.*"

She couldn't get warm and she couldn't stop shaking. It was as though she were slowly freezing from the inside out. The ground was hard beneath her and the cloak only kept out the chill of the morning air but did nothing to warm her. Nicole turned onto her side and tucked her knees up into her chest, trying to block out the vision she had had.

She had seen Eli, and a voice inside her had told her that he was still alive. How could that be? Hadn't he, Michael, and Jer died in the fire? If he was alive, Michael might be too. They could be the evil the others had seen sweeping like a plague across the continent.

She should warn Amanda and Holly. They had a right to know. If it was true then they needed to be prepared. *I should be with them.* She pounded her fist against her thigh. *I don't want to go back. I don't want any part of the magic.*

A voice inside her head mocked her, telling her she was a fool to think that she could ever escape the magic. It had followed her. No, it was in her. She couldn't change that no matter how far she ran.

And what of that other face? She had felt the evil oozing from every pore of the lionesque features. And that voice, *"I shall marry you, Nicole Cahors."* Who was he and how did he know who she was?

She stared down at the bandage wrapping her burned palm. Philippe had told her that within twelve hours there wouldn't even be a mark.

A stray cat that had been lurking close by for the

last hour approached quietly. Its fur was dusty and tangled, and its eyes held a feral gleam. It crept close and finally curled up so that it was touching Nicole's chest. She dropped her hand upon the cat's back.

It purred, startling them both. It settled, though, and stared at her with great almond-shaped eyes. "What am I going to do?"

The cat blinked at her once before squeezing its eyes closed and falling asleep.

SEVEN

SEED MOON

☾

Brains and blood, tissue and bone
Time to reap the death we've sown
Sun above and stones in hand
Help us spread fear throughout the land

Come and see through scrying stone
The plans they make against the Crone
Cast the runes and we shall see
How to triumph, blessed be

Nicole: Outside Madrid, November

Nicole's dreams were wild, vivid. She struggled against
the man she had seen in her vision. He leered at her,
laughing, always laughing. His mouth gaped open
larger and larger like a cavernous yaw. Flames started
shooting out of it, searing her face with their heat. She
tried to scream, to turn away, but her feet wouldn't
move and only a whisper escaped her lips.

"Nicole, come to me," the voice was soft in her mind.

She was finally able to turn, and she saw Philippe standing several feet away, his hand outstretched to her. She reached for his hand.

Now she awoke, and he was saying something to her.

She turned her head toward the door and there he stood, smiling gravely at her. Something warm, like a gentle touch, brushed against her mind, and she smiled. He moved to her and sat down beside her. He took her hand in his and warmth flowed through her.

"We have talked. We will do everything in our power to protect you." He added, "You have a great destiny, Nicole."

Tears stung her eyes. Maybe she had once believed that; it seemed long ago, back when her mother had been alive and they had practiced simple magics together. *But I thought I was going to become a great actress, not a witch!* Now she had nothing. Holly, maybe, had a great destiny, but not her.

"I think you've mistaken me for someone else," she said, dropping her gaze.

With his free hand he tilted her head up so that her eyes met his. "We are not mistaken, Nicole Cahors. You have a great destiny. I know it. I feel it."

She stared deep into his eyes and felt all her barriers falling one by one. She began to cry in earnest, and he wrapped his arms around her, holding her, loving her as all the pain washed through her. His body shuddered slightly at each new wave, as though her pain, memories, and fears were assaulting him as well. When at last she looked up, she saw tears streaming down his face. His lips were moving as though in silent prayer.

He opened his eyes, and she could barely believe, let alone trust, what she saw shining in their depths.

"There's so much I want to tell you," she whispered.

"I know, I can feel it." He bent slowly and kissed her on each cheek.

"I'm not a saint," she said, dipping her head.

He put his hand under her chin and lifted her face back to his. "If you were, we'd have problems. Oh, not that we don't have a few already."

She smiled at his joke even as his touch sent her pulse skittering out of control. She fought down her emotions. There was something she had to do.

"I need to make a phone call."

He nodded as though he had been expecting that. "It has to be short," he warned. "They have been casting their nets trying to find you. We will need to be very fast and very clever."

She nodded and then put her head back against his

chest. All the forces of hell might be looking for her, but for the moment she felt safe.

José Luís had not slept since the vision. When the others had pressed him about it, he had answered in vagaries. Nothing about the vision had been vague, though. He knew even the moment of his death. He also knew there was nothing he could do to avoid it. That didn't mean he wasn't going to try.

This was the fourth place they had been to in search of a phone for Nicole. They needed to avoid the towns, so they had been approaching villas. Within a mile of each they had turned away, sensing something amiss. They were running out of time, though. They could all feel it. Traveling by day was dangerous because of the increased numbers of people, the increased risk of being seen by the wrong person.

He glanced up at the sun as it approached the horizon. Being about during the day, though, had posed less risk than the night would. It was going to be a full moon.

He gazed along the cobblestone street. This tiny village might be their last chance to find a phone before night closed in. Pablo came up next to him. He placed his hand on the boy's head.

"There is a phone next to the café in the square."

José Luís nodded. Something didn't seem quite right here, but he couldn't place his finger on it. He glanced again at the setting sun. There wasn't much time left. They'd have to take the risk.

He began to walk and felt the others falling in behind him. Armand cloaked them so that the villagers would not mark the passage of so many people.

They reached the phone, and Philippe and Nicole began to place the call. The rest of them spread out. José Luís kept one eye on the square and one eye on Philippe and Nicole. He could see the bond that was forming between them and he couldn't help but approve. Philippe was strong and had a stability that Nicole lacked and needed. With his strength and her fire they could make a mark on the world.

It looked as if they had been connected. He smiled tightly. Only magic could allow an international phone call to go through that quickly from a pay phone in a small village.

Nicole's hand shook as she dialed. What was the number? She'd lived in that house all her life, and now when she needed it she couldn't even remember the phone number. Slowly, digit by digit, it came. At last she got through and the phone began to ring.

The answering machine picked up and she hung

up in frustration. She breathed a prayer of thanks to the Goddess when she remembered Amanda's cell phone number. She picked up the phone and dialed.

"Hello?" She nearly wept with joy when she heard her sister's voice on the line.

"Amanda, it's me. Listen carefully."

"Nicole! Nicole, oh, my God! Where are you?"

"In Spain, somewhere, I think. That's not important now, though. You have to listen to me. Eli is still alive."

"Nicki, the *ferry*!"

"Listen to me, Manda." She looked around anxiously. "Eli is still alive."

"But . . . how do you know?"

"I had a vision. It's complicated. But he's alive, and there's big evil happening." Nicole swallowed. "I'm sorry I left, Amanda. Hecate . . ."

"She's fine. Oh, *Nicole*." Amanda was sobbing in earnest now.

Philippe gestured at her to hurry. She took a breath. "Did something happen to Holly?"

"Eddie's dead!"

"What about Holly?" Nicole almost shouted.

"She saved me. I would have died. Nicki, oh, please, Nicki, come home. We need you."

"I—I will," Nicole said firmly. Now Philippe

waved his hands and shook his head, silently urging her to get off the phone. "I have to go."

"No!" Amanda wailed.

"I have to," she said firmly. "I'll try to call again soon."

Hating herself, she hung up.

Nicole looked very upset. José Luís was concerned, watching, unable to hear what she was saying. At last she hung up, and Philippe gathered her close. José Luís took a step toward them. The sooner they left, the better.

Searing pain exploded in his back and chest. He crumbled to his knees, trying to shout. No sound came out. He twisted as he fell, landing on his back and driving the knife further into his punctured lung.

As he stared up into the face of his killer, he could see the moon, pale and full already, visible in the sky above.

As the world went black he thought, *Ay, Dios mío, the visions never lie.*

"I shouldn't have left. I should never have left," Nicole murmured against Philippe's chest as they walked away from the phone booth.

"Ah, petite," Philippe whispered "I am so sorry."

They turned toward José Luís.

Nicole gasped as she saw the dark figure looming behind him.

Then José Luís fell to the ground, stricken.

From everywhere, menacing hooded figures appeared, as though rising from the very earth. Their cloaks were so dark they seemed to absorb the last vestiges of light around them. One rose behind Philippe, and Nicole shouted a warning.

He turned to face it just as the others of the coven exploded onto the scene. Armand shot into motion, a spinning whirlwind of magic and death. The last ray of the dying sun glinted off the sword he wielded. Nicole's shocked mind wondered briefly where it had come from. The man twisted and turned like a fiend, chanting, shouting curses, and swinging the deadly blade. Three dark figures fell. More surged up to take their place.

From the top of a nearby roof, Nicole heard a loud, keening wail. She glanced up to see Pablo. He slowly extended his hands; bright light suddenly seemed to engulf his body. It shot through his fingers and cast the entire square in a blue, unearthly glow. The dark figures squealed and tried to scuttle away from the light.

Suddenly a hand clasped her upper arm and yanked her backward. A moment later another creature appeared where she had been standing. Alonzo kept hold of her arm but took a step forward. He thrust a crucifix toward the creature's face.

"Ego te expello in nomine Christi."

The creature shrieked and dissolved before her eyes. She looked from Alonzo to the cross held in his outstretched hand.

"Hey, whatever works." He shrugged. "It was a demon." He gestured up to where Pablo continued to illuminate the scene. "They have more cause to fear Light than we do. Problem is, not all of these things are demons."

Alonzo spun away at a call from Armand. The younger man was surrounded by cloaked figures brandishing swords of their own. The bluish light flickered for a moment and Nicole glanced upward nervously. Pablo's strength was fading. Maybe she could get up on the roof and help him.

Her scalp began to tingle, and she twisted just in time to sidestep a dark figure rushing her. Demon or something else? She couldn't tell, but she could feel power begin to surge through her. She summoned a fireball. If it was human it would burn. If it was demon it would feel right at home. The thing turned just in time for the fireball to explode in its chest. A deep laugh came from it and set her hair on end. It took a step forward and she braced herself.

A ball of bright blue light burst through the creature's chest, and it stood for only a moment, staring, before it dissipated into smoke. Behind where the creature had stood was Philippe. He gave her a small smile before turning to battle two other demons who had been trying to sneak up on him.

She moved to help him. Just then Pablo's light was extinguished, and the entire square was plunged into darkness. Nicole whispered a spell to help her vision, but it only helped slightly.

Arms wrapped hard around her, lifting her, shrieking into the air. She opened her lips to scream a spell, but a strong hand clamped over her nose and mouth, shutting off her air. She struggled, trying to break free, but her attacker was too strong. As her strength was fading, she managed to twist around. The figure's hood had fallen back to reveal a familiar face, the face she had seen in her dreams.

As the world went black, the last thing she heard was Philippe's voice echoing in her mind. *"I will find you, Nicole. I will track you through heaven and hell if I must."*

Amanda, Nicole, Kari: Seattle, November

Tante Cecile, Silvana, and Tommy—who had not been called to attend the meeting on the ferry—found Holly and Amanda at the hospital. Like so many of the other survivors, they had been herded into a private conference room in the hospital away from the throngs of news media demanding eyewitness accounts, demanding to know exactly what had happened on the dark waters.

The place was in chaos—people in blankets crying, other people shouting, some sitting in numb silence on padded conference chairs or the additional gray metal folding chairs that had been brought in. On the conference room table were urns of coffee and trays of sandwiches.

Ensconced in their own little corner of the room, the two *voudon* enfolded the witches in their arms; all of them wept for Eddie.

Then Nicole called Amanda—whose cell phone, miraculously, had stayed in her jeans pocket and survived the ordeal in the water, as the little case she kept it in was waterproof—and told her about Eli.

Uncle Richard phoned from the hospital parking lot to say that it was a mob scene and that he would get to them as quickly as he could. He had no recollection of his possession, and Holly and Amanda agreed to keep it that way.

Kialish showed. Dan could not be reached. It fell to Holly to deliver the blow of Eddie's death. Kialish fell apart, thanked her, and told her he was so very glad that she and Amanda had survived.

She felt awful; she had not told him that she had abandoned Eddie to the monsters. *That I could have saved him. I picked Amanda . . . and I didn't even know if she was still alive.*

"Why did you tell us to go?" Holly shouted at Tante Cecile, deflecting her guilt on to the other woman. "To meet on *water*?"

Tante Cecile flashed with anger. "Of course I didn't, Holly! You were set up! All of us!"

"But . . ." Amanda wiped her eyes. "But you called me."

Tante Cecile shook her head. "I didn't."

The two witch cousins stared long and hard at each other. "Michael," Holly said, her jaw set.

"It sounded exactly like you," Amanda murmured. "How can he do that?"

"Same way we do so much of what we do," Silvana cut in, her arm around Eddie's stricken lover. His face was gray; in the last five minutes, he seemed to have aged twenty years. "With magic."

"Maybe that's why I wasn't called," Tommy said. "Michael doesn't know I hang out with you guys."

Tears rolled down Kialish's cheeks. "Holly . . ." His

shoulders heaved and he began to sob. "Tell me it was a quick death."

She swallowed hard. "Yes. He didn't even see it."

Oh, Goddess, forgive me.

A woman in bright tropical scrubs scuttled over and put her arm around Kialish, saying, "Do you need something, sir?"

He shook his head, utterly defeated. Like a very old man, he let her lead him to a chair. She bustled off and got him a sandwich and a blanket. He stared down at them as if he had never seen such alien objects in his life.

Silvana put her hands on his shoulders, closed her eyes, and began a quiet incantation.

Tante Cecile turned to Amanda and Holly. "You see how he works against us," she said. "How important it is for us to stick together." She gazed levelly at Holly. "And why you have to remain the High Priestess. Your power is stronger than Amanda's."

"Nicole's coming home," Amanda added. "We'll be the three again."

Holly felt as if she had swallowed a stone. She said, "But Jer and I . . . our power combined is even stronger. It's unbelievably strong."

The others stared at her in disbelief.

"Don't you dare leave us, Holly!" Amanda shouted at her.

Tommy went to Amanda's side, slid his arm around her waist in that defending way boyfriends—not best friends—did. Despite her distraction, Holly took note of that.

"He's going to win if we don't get some help," Holly shot back. She tried to keep her voice calm. Taking a few deep breaths, she said, "I know this so deeply in my soul, Manda. I have to save him. My power merged with his can defeat his father."

"You don't know that! You can't know that!" Amanda shouted. Heads turned in their direction. "You're just like us, figuring all this stuff out as we go along!"

"Shh, Manda," Tommy cautioned. "He might have spies around. We have to be discreet."

Silvana raised a hand. "I'm taking Kialish home," she announced.

That stopped the argument. The three took in Kialish's disheveled appearance, his bereft, lost expression, and the heat among them simply evaporated. Tommy kept his arm around Amanda, and Amanda let it stay there.

"Good," Tante Cecile said, obviously proud of her daughter. "Be careful. Very careful."

"We're not the ones he's after," Silvana said.

Holly felt another rush of shame. *I will kill them one by one. I carry the curse. Will I take it to Jer? Will I kill him, too?*

I have to go to him. I know it. And I know it's not Michael leading me to him. . . .

At the window of the hospital conference room, Fantasme, spirit familiar of the Deveraux, screeched and flapped his wings. He had just come to Michael from England, magically flying to Seattle in a split-second to his master's side.

The bird flew toward the moon, bathing himself in its rays, turning his shiny black body this way and that.

Then he swooped down into the utter confusion of the hospital parking structure, landing on the outstretched arm of Michael Deveraux, who had been waiting for him.

Bird eye gazed into warlock eye, and Michael saw everything that Fantasme had. He nodded.

"Time for mischief," he told the bird.

With a wave of his hand, he parted the crowd in front of him. They moved without realizing it; he had a clear path that no one else noticed.

He strode down the stairs, disdaining the elevator. Cameras did not aim his way; reporters did not see him. No one saw him, or the huge, magical creature that perched on his arm.

At the foot of the stairs, near a bush, he snapped his fingers.

The imp emerged, its fanged mouth grinning broadly, its eyes shining with glee. Michael was put in mind of Ariel, from Shakespeare's *The Tempest*.

The creature bobbled along beside Michael, gazing up at him with eagerness. It said, "What are we doing?"

"We're up to no good," Michael informed him.

They sauntered along, three figures who could have been alone in the forest, for all the attention anyone paid to them. Then Michael uttered a finder's spell and closed his eyes, seeing in his mind the covenates of Holly Cathers.

The ones named Silvana and Kialish were being escorted by an overly cheerful woman in Hawaiian-motif scrubs, who was vainly trying to get them to take sandwiches with them. Michael shook his head, marveling at her inappropriate behavior. The boy had just lost his lover, for God's sake.

Continuing on his unobstructed walkabout, Michael and his companions began to head toward the same exit, down the side of the hospital, stepping over the cables where TV crews had set up their equipment, observing the emotional after-effects of his attack on the ferry.

It was a good piece of work, he thought. *I'll be censured for it, no doubt, for performing magic in a public place.*

A TV reporter was standing in front of a camera, delivering her version of what had happened.

"A lost gray whale caused an uproar earlier this evening," she began, "when it accidentally tipped over a ferry. Compounding the tragedy, a school of sharks attacked the hapless passengers, all of whom could have been saved by the Coast Guard vessels that sped to the side of the stricken vessel, if only they could have swum more quickly to safety. . . ."

Some will remember what really happened, he thought. *Others will talk themselves out of it.*

Either way, Sir William will not be pleased. But there's not much he can do about it. He wants the Black Fire.

They were almost at the exit door—both he and his companions, and Silvana and Kialish. Grief was making them sloppy; the wards they had set around themselves would be simple to neutralize.

He did so with a few incantations and gestures of his hands.

Then the exit door opened, and he planted himself rather dramatically in front of it.

"Hi," he said to the startled pair.

Silvana opened her mouth; whether to shout or scream—*or say hi back*—he had no idea.

The imp darted forward and leaped at her, both its fists doubled, and slammed them into her face. Kialish would have shouted then, except that Michael aimed a glowing ball of energy at him, and it knocked him out.

The two tumbled to the floor.

Michael stepped around them to an empty gurney pushed against the wall, wheeled it back, and loaded the two on it, Kialish first and then Silvana on top of him, like cord wood.

Whistling to himself, he wheeled them outside.

No one noticed. No one tried to stop him.

She'll be madder than a wet hen, he thought, delighted. *And they won't let her leave to find my son.*

The falcon threw back its head and laughed. The imp joined in, cackling madly. Michael only smiled.

EIGHT

PLANTING MOON

Fear us now our power grows
Strength to vanquish all our foes
Will to crush and might to maim
We'll not rest till they are slain

Growing, swelling, fill the night
Shine upon us with thy light
Blessed moon above us give
Guidance now on how to live

Nicole: En route to London, November

Nicole awoke feeling as if she was going to throw up.
She was lying down and was being bounced all around.
She lay still, trying to suppress the nausea as her brain
raced trying to figure out where she was.

She seemed to be reclining in the back seat of a car;
she tried to sit up but couldn't. Her arms and legs felt
constricted, and she craned her neck trying to look at
her legs and finally caught a glimpse of ropes.

It all came flooding back to her. The battle, the hand over her mouth and nose, the leering face.

And, most of all, Philippe's voice telling her he'd be coming for her.

In a whisper she commanded the knots to loosen. A stabbing pain shot through her skull, but the ropes didn't budge. She blinked hard against the pain and tried again. Nothing except more pain.

A voice laughed hard and low. "Forget about it. You're bound tight both physically and magically."

Eli. A wave of hate washed through her being. Eli was behind this. *Of course.*

But what about the other man, the one from her vision? How did he fit into all of this?

She bounced painfully as the car hit a pothole. Her stomach twisted even more fiercely. The car turned suddenly to the right, and the top of her head smacked against the door. The car stopped hard, and she went flying into the back of the front seats and fell, wedged into the space between them and the back seat.

Disgusted, she lay waiting for assistance. Several minutes passed before the back doors finally opened. Eli chuckled cruelly.

"That can't be comfortable."

She bit back a retort, refusing to rise to his baiting. He picked up her feet and someone else grabbed her shoulders. They threw her up onto the seat. Then Eli grasped her ankles and began to pull her from the car. The friction burned her legs. She was more concerned, though, about her shirt as it began to bunch up around her bra. Finally her feet hit the ground, and with Eli's help she struggled to a sitting position. He grabbed a fistful of her shirt and pulled her up and out of the car to a standing position.

The other man came around the car and his eyes caught and held her. He bent and put his shoulder into her pelvis and rose. She folded in half over his back, feeling helpless and angry as he carried her like a sack of potatoes. Her chin banged painfully against his back, and she felt a little better when he winced.

The small building reminded Nicole of the safe houses she had visited with José Luís's coven. The floor here, though, was covered with dirt, and the furniture was of a cruder make. She'd refused the chair that her captors had offered her, choosing to stand instead. It made her feel more in control, even if it was just an illusion. Eli and the other man conferred together for several minutes, speaking in hushed tones. At last the stranger turned to her.

"Just kill me and get it over with," she said.

Nicole winced as the words sounded hollow even

to her. She'd been trying for defiance, a fierce, fearless declaration of her will. Instead it sounded like the helpless, pitiful cry of a victim who feared her captor's intentions more than death.

His lips twisted in a cruel sneer. He stepped closer to her, so close he was nearly touching her. He met her eyes, and she forced herself to stare back.

"Maybe I will. Probably I won't."

The words hung in the air between them, half-threat, half-promise. Something cold and hard glittered in his eyes: the look of the predator eyeing his prey and imagining the taste of it.

She lifted her chin higher, another instinctive act of defiance. By exposing her throat she showed no fear, at least in theory. A wolflike smile turned the corners of his lips up, and he bared his teeth ever so slightly. His eyes bored deeper into hers, conveying his hate, his contempt, and something more.

He stepped back abruptly and turned away growling, but it was too late. She had seen that which he did not want her to. Aside from the cruelty, the rage, and the evil, she had seen curiosity.

She could work with that.

She quietly tested the ropes that bound her both physically and psychically. There was no give. Holly would be able to escape these bonds. Holly might even be able to take on both Eli and the other man by now, if her strength had grown. But there was something Holly couldn't do that Nicole could.

When he next glanced her way she held his eyes and smiled. His eyes narrowed, but he didn't turn away.

Emboldened, she asked, "Who are you?"

Pride crackled in his voice as he answered, "I am James, son of Sir William Moore, and heir to the throne of the Supreme Coven."

"Supreme Coven? Is that supposed to mean something to me?"

He growled low in his throat. "It should, witch. If you had half a brain you would be trembling in fear from the very mention of it."

She allowed herself a smile. "Sorry. Never heard of it, your dad, or you."

He moved quickly toward her, and for a moment she thought she might have pushed too hard. He raised a hand as though to strike her, but instead twisted his fingers in her hair and yanked her face close to his.

"You'll wish you still hadn't, by the time my father is through with you."

Sleep did not come easily that night. She was stretched out on the hard dirt floor with her cheek to the earth. The two men took turns sleeping, and she could feel their eyes upon her. When at last she did fall asleep, it was only to be awakened minutes later by a rough hand on her shoulder.

"Time to move," Eli informed her gruffly.

At least they permitted her to sit upright in the back seat of the car, although her arms remained tightly bound. She was tired enough that she found herself drifting off to sleep, jarred awake every so often by another pothole in the road.

She was exhausted by the time they stopped for the night. The small shack was little better than the one they'd stayed at the night before. At least this one had cots.

The men produced bread and cheese from somewhere, and Nicole hoped briefly that they might untie her. The hope was in vain, though. Eli fed her while James paced. In between bites she managed to ask, "How come we're taking so long to get wherever it is we're going?"

"This is the quickest way, considering. Our magic's strong, but it would be difficult to keep an entire airport full of people—not to mention plane passengers—from realizing you were our prisoner. Unnecessary, anyway. Two more days and we'll be where we need to go," James answered, barely breaking step.

Eli stuffed another mouthful of bread into her

mouth, and Nicole glanced at him, loathing him as she did herself. She couldn't believe she'd ever been attracted to his dark nature. She had been so foolish to believe that she could tame him. As though sensing her thoughts, he gave her the same twisted smile he used to give her when he was touching her, when he was . . .

He began to undress her with his eyes and she turned away, disgusted. Her eyes fell on the pacing James, and a thought struck her.

Sex is Eli's weakness. Always has been, even before me.

She turned her head slowly, deliberately, back to Eli and batted her eyelashes once, twice. *Easy, don't overdo it.* She smiled and gazed at him suggestively. She gave him her best come-hither look and watched him lick his lips nervously as he glanced toward James.

In the days they'd been together, careful observation had led her to believe that while Eli feared James somewhat, he didn't respect him. Now he glanced back at her, shifting his weight, probably completely unaware of his body language.

Okay, I'm gonna go for it . . . with both of them.

James was an unknown factor, but Eli she knew well. Eli could be counted on to want whatever someone else had. She dropped her eyes to keep him from knowing that the blush mounting her cheeks was not from old days and old memories, but from shame.

She put the whammy on James same as Eli, and he rose to the bait. Soon he was glancing her way, displaying his interest, and Eli was reacting. Without realizing it, the two warlocks were circling her, each with an eye on the other.

She was thrilled, triumphant . . . and a little smug about all those years Amanda had chided her about worrying about what guys thought of her.

When we get back together, I'm going to have to tell Holly and Amanda about this. And we're going to have to read up on sex magic.

That's what all this has been about—Michael seducing Mom, and this whole Jean and Isabeau deal; having a High Priestess and a guy with a "long arm." *Excuse me? A "long arm"?*

After two days the magic bonds had loosened ever so slightly. She had a chance to try something more, a spell small enough that it would not register with the two men. A spell small enough to be covered by the magical energy already flowing about them. Something very small.

She breathed the glamour into life, something to make her even more beautiful and, Goddess willing, completely irresistible.

By dinner James had untied her. And his nearness

excited her; she couldn't deny that. His smoldering looks shot a tingle down to the small of her back.

By breakfast even she was having a hard time remembering that the electricity between them was one of her glamours.

"What is your father going to do to me?" she asked James as they shared a bottle of wine with Eli.

James shrugged nonchalantly. "Kill you, I guess. You are, after all, a Cahors."

"And you are a Moore," she said, "creator of the Supreme Coven chicken sandwich." It had become something of a joke between them.

Grinning, he nodded and took a swig of wine.

"It doesn't have to be this way," she murmured.

He laughed dangerously low as he handed her the bottle. "What's in a name, eh, Rosebud?"

"You're a movie fan." She took the wine and threw some back. Her hands were shaking; she was terrified.

But I'm still alive.

"I'm a movie fan," he said agreeably, but there was flint in his gaze.

I'm not safe, though. I'm not safe at all.

She's a hottie.

James didn't trust her. He'd be lying, though, if he

didn't admit he was attracted to her. Everyone had heard the rumors of Cahors-Deveraux power. It clearly hadn't worked for Nicole and Eli. Maybe it had nothing to do with houses. Maybe it was all about a certain combination of witch and warlock. House Moore was more powerful now than House Deveraux. Maybe leadership was essential. He licked his lips as he imagined an alliance that could bring him even more power.

With Cahors magic aligned with his, he couldn't fail to overthrow his father.

Hmm . . .

He looked into her eyes and couldn't trust what he saw shining there. *She wants me . . . or else she's really good at faking it.*

Okay, maybe the little bitch was playing him. Then again, maybe she wasn't. He wasn't a bad package; and oh, yeah, baby, speaking of packages . . .

He glanced over at Eli and saw the other man eyeing Nicole. A quick burst of anger made him tremble.

You had your shot. Now back off.

A voice from somewhere seemed to be whispering in his ear, *"It's all about the power. That's what she likes. You have it. He doesn't."*

"She wants to feel your power, James.

"That's what she wants. Your power.

"You.

"No need to kill her. . . . No need at all.

"You can have her. She wants you.

"You, James. You can have a Cahors witch."

James smiled slowly as he wrapped an arm around Nicole's waist. She put her hand over his and gave him such a look that it was hard to restrain himself from taking her right then and there.

But that Deveraux nerd Eli was around somewhere, and it wasn't a good idea to provoke a fight with a potential ally, especially while they were traveling together.

We'll be in England soon.

And I think I just might have a little surprise for my father.

King James I: En route to England from Denmark, 1589

Below decks, at the threshold of their royal quarters, the king of Scotland surveyed his bride, whom he was bringing home to Scotland. She was beautiful. She was a few years younger than he, but her mind had been honed by an inquisitive nature, and she had the bearing of someone older. Her heavily embroidered white skirts were lovely, and the black jacket she wore was just as elegant.

He stared down at the decorative roses on his shoes that hid the laces, and lost himself in thoughts of her beauty. Few men had the privilege to marry such a woman, and he would do everything in his power to make her happy.

Finally he looked up and leaned close to Anne, a smile playing across his features. "I think I shall write a poem about your eyes."

She blushed fiercely. "You've already written me a dozen poems."

"Yes, but not one exclusively devoted to those magnificent pools of light that reflect the beauty and purity of your soul."

She laughed in an embarrassed manner, but he could tell by the way she glowed that she was secretly pleased. "We've only half a day until we reach port. Surely the king of Scotland, and one day of England, can find better ways to occupy his time than writing love poetry?"

He took her hand in his and gazed into her eyes. "Nothing is more important to the king than his queen. Has not God commanded us that love is our highest duty? And as a husband I am to care for you as Christ does His faithful ones. Therefore, how could I be trusted to rule a country if I cannot follow God's simplest decrees? How can I rule thousands with compassion if I gaze upon your exquisite face and am not moved to poetry?"

She smiled. "James, I love your poetry. I just wish all you wrote was as pleasant to read."

He patted her hand. "You're referencing the daemonologies that I am penning."

She shuddered. "Such horrible, frightening things."

"Dearest Anne, not all the world is as beautiful as you. This world is filled with terrifying things, both demons and the wretched persons who serve them. It is our duty to dispel the myths and denials surrounding such creatures. We must shine the light of truth upon those that live in darkness."

She shook her head slowly. "Some of it just seems so fantastical."

"Which? Demons or witches?"

She never had a chance to respond. The ship lurched violently sideways. James and Anne were thrown hard against the bulkhead; from the ladderway, water cascaded from the deck and spilled around their ankles.

Shouts of alarm issued from all quarters of the ship.

"Courage, my darling," James shouted as he moved forward toward the ladderway. His thought was to get them on deck, above the water line, where they would be safer.

After listing on its side for what seemed an eternity, the vessel straightened back out.

"Anne, now!" James shouted, slogging through the rising water.

"I can't! My skirts!"

He turned to look at her. Her splendid dress was not only ruined, it was killing her. The skirts held too much water; she could never swim in them. If they had to abandon the vessel, the weight of them would drag her down like a stone to her death.

Barely thinking, he fought his way into the next compartment and picked up his sword from where it had fallen to the floor. The water was waist deep as he made his way back to Anne.

Unsheathing the weapon, he began hacking at her skirts until he was able to cut most of it off. She stood shivering in her undergarments, staring at him with frightened eyes. He grabbed her hand and pulled her out of the cabin. They were halfway up the stairs when the ship lurched again.

He kept going, clinging to her hand, pulling her when he had to. They made it to the deck just as a wave crashed over it. It swept them both into the water. He kicked hard to the surface, Anne still clinging to his hand and kicking along with him. His lungs began to burn from lack of oxygen.

Just when he thought that all was lost, they broke the surface. Air rushed into his lungs, and he gasped and coughed. He twisted around scanning the water. A small boat stood a ways off, and they began swimming toward it, rain pelting their faces.

When they came alongside, hands reached down and pulled them up into the boat. Anxious fisherman scanned their faces and asked them if they were hurt. Slowly James shook his head. He turned to look back toward his ship.

All that was still visible of the royal vessel was her bow, and even as he watched, it slipped beneath the dark waves. As suddenly as it had risen, the storm dissipated.

The captain of the fishing boat crossed himself. "I've never seen anything like it."

"How so?" James questioned sharply.

"The squall. She came out of nowhere. It was like she was alive, passing us to attack your ship. God have mercy."

Eyes hard, James turned back to Anne. "Do you still doubt the presence of witches?"

These Witches . . . can rayse stormes and tempestes in the aire, either upon sea or land, though not universally, but in such a particular place and prescribed boundes, as God will permitte them so to trouble: Which likewise is verie easie to be discerned from anie other naturall tempestes that are meteores, in respect of the suddaine and violent raising thereof, together with the short induring of the same.

The king put his pen down and pressed his fingers to his temples.

His trusted advisor waited patiently. The man knew not to interrupt while James was writing. Finally James looked up wearily. "Any word about the identity of the hags who tried to kill the queen and me?"

After months of negative replies, he had grown to fear he would never discover the responsible ones. He had, however, had some small success in rousting some witches and casting light on the dark places wherein they dwelled.

"Yes, Your Majesty," the man said, clearly pleased with himself. "A gentleman would like to speak with you privately. He claims to have knowledge of the witch who attacked you."

James blinked in surprise. *Could it really be?* His fatigue forgotten, he commanded, "Show him in and make certain no one disturbs us."

His aid bowed and left. Within moments he ushered a tall, dark-haired man into the chamber, then left, closing the door behind him.

"Your Majesty," the stranger greeted, dropping to one knee.

James gestured for the man to rise, leaning forward eagerly to hear what he had to say "Rise, good sir. Tell me who you are and why you have come."

The man did as he was ordered, but bowed his head with great humility and announced, "My name is Luc Deveraux, Your Majesty. I am here because I have come to understand that we have a common enemy."

James lifted a brow. "And who might this unfortunate be?"

"She is called Barbara Cahors."

The king was mildly disappointed. That was no one whom he knew. "The name means nothing to me."

"It will soon, your majesty," Luc Deveraux said earnestly, his expression one of great concern and steadfastness, "for she is the witch that of late tried to kill your good lady and yourself."

James leaned forward farther, eyeing the other man intently. *This is exactly what I have been wanting to hear. And so, I needs must doubt it. Courtiers thrive on pleasing me . . . or rather, appearing to please me.*

With great sternness of tone, he said, "How do I know that you do not have some personal vendetta against this woman and thereby seek to bring her to ruin by my hand?"

"But I *do* have a personal grievance," Deveraux

assured him. "That I do, sir, and I stand by my accusation."

The king and queen both attended the burning of the witches. Barbara Cahors and her handmaid had been lashed to great pyres, found guilty of the crimes of witchcraft and the attempted murder of the royal couple. Luc Deveraux was also present, close enough that Barbara could see him, far enough away that she could not easily identify him to the soldiers guarding her.

A smirk touched his face as he watched the hem of her skirt catch fire. Soon the witch would burn, like so many innocent women had before her. Barbara was far from innocent, though. He had traced her to this place with great effort. Spies and magic spells had revealed to him all the remaining members of the Cahors Coven. Barbara was one of several whom he planned to kill. The destruction of his enemy brought him great joy. Perhaps at last the House of Deveraux would be rid of the House of Cahors.

His victory was not entirely complete, though. Barbara's young daughter, Cassandra, had escaped, and though he had combed the countryside, he had been unable to find the child. Without her mother to train her, though, the girl might never come to fully realize her powers. Regardless if she lived or died, the back of House Cahors was broken, and Deveraux was ascendant.

James: London, November

At the headquarters of the Supreme Coven, Sir William looked up as his son, James, strode into the room. The young man stood before him, barely paying the proper respect. Excitement and arrogance streamed from the young pup like musk.

"Father."

"So, you have returned. Were you successful?"

James smiled. "More than expected."

He turned, and a young woman was escorted into the hall. Though her hands were bound behind her, she bore herself with grace, standing tall. Sir William breathed deeply. He could smell the fear coming off her, but otherwise she masked it well.

"Father, allow me to introduce Nicole Anderson, my fiancée."

Holly: Seattle, November

After Silvana and Kialish left the hospital, Holly, Amanda, Tommy, and Kari stood around awkwardly, angrily, very much at odds with one another. No one spoke. Tommy looked on helplessly, unable to comfort Amanda or the other two.

It fell to Tante Cecile to break the silence. She said to the others, "We must hold a Circle and ask the Goddess our best course of action—whether or not Holly should go to save Jeraud. We have the ability to seek guidance, and we should."

Holly's lips parted to protest. *What if she says no?* It occurred to her that although she had served as High Priestess for months, she had not really yielded herself to the Goddess. She had looked on the success of their magic spells almost the same as if they had been performing successful lab experiments in chemistry class. The thought of laying down her will was terrifying.

Tante Cecile looked straight at her as if she was reading her thoughts. Slowly she nodded. "You have just reached the threshold," she said. "You're on the brink of truly reclaiming your birthright, Holly."

Holly swallowed hard. Her chest was so tight she couldn't breathe. Amanda frowned, puzzled, and Kari said anxiously, "What are you two talking about? You're speaking in secret code."

A great fear washed over Holly. In the midst of the chaos and confusion, she was overwhelmed. *If I do this—agree to really put myself in Her hands—I will be different for the rest of my life. What if my Goddess is a ruthless lady? What if allegiance to her is what made the Cahors before me so brutal?*

"It's still your choice," Tante Cecile said. "You can turn back."

"We'll give Kialish tonight to grieve," Holly said. "Then we'll hold Circle tomorrow night and I'll go before the Goddess." She said to Amanda, "I can't let you lead the coven. It's my responsibility."

"You still can't go to him," Amanda said icily in reply. Tommy put his arm on her shoulder, and this time she shrugged it off, as if she weren't really paying attention to what he was doing and needed to be left alone.

His look of disappointment spoke volumes to Holly.

"We'll ask the Goddess what to do," Tante Cecile soothed. "We'll have a Clearing and a Knowing." She sighed. "If we're lucky."

Amanda and Kari both moved a bit away, Kari folding her arms. She was still an outsider, still not fully committed to sharing her lot with the others. And she loved Jer, and hated Holly for leaving him to burn in the Black Fire.

"Tonight," Tante Cecile said, "we should stick together. Whose house should we sleep in?"

"Girls! Thank God you're all right!"

Uncle Richard hurried across the threshold of the conference room as the ever-helpful woman in bright scrubs pointed the four out to him. His face was radiant with relief; he looked more alive than Holly had seen him since Aunt Marie-Claire's death.

"Daddy!" Amanda cried, and raced toward him.

"I think we should go to their house," Kari said, and Tommy nodded. "Richard won't want Amanda to go out again, and I sure as hell don't want to hold Circle at my place."

Holly nodded, agreeing.

Tante Cecile pulled her cell phone out of her purse and punched in a number. She waited, murmuring, "Come on, Sylvie, pick up. Ah." She brightened. "Sylvie, it's Mom. Listen—"

She caught her breath, her eyes widening. Then she gasped. "No," she whispered. "No!"

Holly grabbed the phone out of her hand and pressed it against her ear.

"If you want to see her again, you'll give up Holly to me," a voice was saying.

Michael. He's kidnapped Silvana.

Tante Cecile sought refuge in Kari's arms, who, though not a warm person, enfolded her in a strong embrace and asked, "What's going on?"

"Do you have Kialish, too?" Holly demanded.

"Oh, no," Kari whispered. "He's kidnapped them?"

Tante Cecile shut her eyes tightly and began to chant in French.

"Why, Ms. Cathers, how nice to hear your voice," said Michael with syrupy sarcasm. "Of course I have Kialish, too. Do you know where his father is? Because I've tried repeatedly to reach him."

"Where do you want to make the exchange?" she said flatly.

Tante Cecile stopped chanting; Kari whispered, "No, you can't do that," but Holly saw the flicker in her eye that said, *Maybe you should, Holly. Maybe that would be payback for Jer.*

"On the water, of course," Michael said, obviously relishing his position.

"When?"

"I would say two nights hence."

"Why not sooner?" Holly asked.

"Patience, Holly." He chuckled. "Oh, and . . ."

"Yes?"

"I probably won't give them back to you alive."

Then he hung up.

Holly and Amanda had still not clued in Uncle Richard, and when the group converged on their house he was unhappy about it. He wanted his daughter and his niece home alone with him, and safe.

After a few minutes of settling in, Tante Cecile wove a spell on him, making him very sleepy. Then she sent him upstairs to go to bed.

Once he was out of the way, she turned to the others.

"We are in a state of siege," Tante Cecile said as she plaited her hair into corn rows, adding beads of silver and turquoise.

The cats patrolled outside, the trio of Cathers witch familiars moving with boldness and stealth. Amanda and Holly had begun to understand what familiars could do, and what they were: magical extensions of a witch's abilities and intentions—confidantes, in a subverbal way, and companions.

As the familiar of a witch who had abandoned her coven, Hecate hung back, deferring slightly to the others. She also tried harder: since then, she hunted birds on the grounds of the Anderson mansion and rodents in their basement with the fervor of a crusader in the Holy Land.

Bast, the familiar of the pivotal witch of the family, reappeared in the living room as if to announce that the perimeter was secured.

It was then that Tante Cecile looked first at her, and then at Holly. Her face clouded; she turned away once, then turned back.

"Holly, in the kitchen?" she asked.

Holly followed her.

Tante Cecile leaned up against the island in the

center of the kitchen and said, "You need to feed the water, child. Your magic will be stronger."

"I'm sorry?" Holly asked, as a chill broke out along her shoulders and up and down her spine. "What do you mean?"

Tante Cecile hesitated. "In the old days, in many religions, there were . . . sacrifices."

"Yes," Holly breathed. "So I've heard."

"Giving something to the water means that you sacrifice it . . . by water."

Holly waited, not getting it. Bast began to weave in and out of her legs, purring and flicking her tail.

"You drown them," Tante Cecile said.

The *voudon* glanced down at Bast, who mewed sweetly at her, then returned to her business of stroking her mistress with her tail.

NINE

NINTH MOON

☾

Nothing now can block our path
The world trembles at our wrath
Murder, kidnap, torture, and lies
Dark hearts beneath darker skies

Crying now within the night
Waiting for the moon's great light
Maiden whispers low and still
Commanding us to go and kill

Holly: Seattle, November

Holly couldn't kill Bast.

So she killed Hecate instead.

She put it from her mind as she did it—the way the beautiful cat stared up at her as she placed her in the bathtub . . .

. . . the way she struggled.

It was as if Holly wasn't really there. She shut herself down completely, neither seeing, nor hearing—not feeling anything. From a hard, dark place in the center of her being, she took the life of Nicole's cat and offered it to darker spirits than she had ever called upon before.

They answered; the act allowed them access, and their presence swept a cold wind through her bones and her heart. From head to toe she was chilled, frightened, and ashamed; she had done something she could never take back, on her knees beside the tub in the darkened bathroom, with one single black candle for company.

Outside the house, Bast and Freya threw back their heads and screamed in fury and despair; they would have wakened the dead, but they could not awaken Amanda and the others, because Holly had put them all into a deep, dreamless sleep. The cats flung themselves at the front door, and at the ground floor windows, livid with her, begging her to stop. Her face a cipher, her heart a stone, she gave to the water something precious, demanding—not asking—the Dark Ones to protect her coven and give her the strength to save Kialish and Silvana.

When it was over, she was different, and she knew she would never be the same again. Her gaze was steadier, her smile less sweet. Ambition and determination had supplanted her goodness; now she had purpose and passion, but she wasn't certain that she was still lovable.

After Hecate was dead, Holly stumbled into her heavily warded bedroom and slept for thirteen hours.

Amanda told her later that she had tried every spell she knew of to awaken her, finally asking Kari and Tommy to go to Kari's for some books she had there, and asking Dan to come and help her and Tante Cecile.

The shaman and the *voudon* had known instantly what she had done, but they didn't tell Amanda. All they told her was to do nothing and let Holly rest.

Holly's dreams were troubled, boiling over with flames and dark waters, monsters that swam out of the chambers of her heart and demons devouring her soul. She dreamed of her parents, waterlogged and dead; she dreamed of Barbara Davis-Chin, still in the hospital and near death. Everyone she loved was cut off from her by a barrier of shiny obsidian black; everyone she hated was pointing at her and laughing.

Then Hecate stared at her from beneath the dirt that Holly had heaped over her in the backyard, the cat whispering, *You crossed the line with my death; you are doomed.*

Over and over the words spilled across her body and crept through her mind: *You sold your soul. . . .*

When Holly awoke, Amanda was standing beside her bed in tears, and a woman with blue-black hair and almond-shaped eyes stood beside her. She was dressed all in black, from a velour turtleneck sweater to a pair of black wool pants. Her skin was very pale and she had on very subtle makeup. Her earrings were silver crescent moons.

Startled to find a stranger in her room, Holly raised herself on one elbow.

Amanda blurted, "Holly, how could you!"

The other woman put a hand on Amanda's arm and said softly, "Amanda, would you get us some tea?"

Amanda frowned, then bobbed her head and dashed from the room.

The woman regarded Holly for a moment. Then she sighed, pulled up a chair, and sat down.

Without preamble, she said bluntly, "You crossed the line."

Holly licked her lips. She was thirsty and still muzzy with sleep. She raked her curls out of her face and sat up against the headboard.

"Who are you?" she asked the woman.

"I'm from the Mother Coven," she told her. "I'm Anne-Louise Montrachet."

Holly looked down at her hands, which were trembling. "No one from the Mother Coven has ever contacted us before," Holly said. "Whatever it is."

"We are a very old and prominent confederation of

covens," she informed her. "We were founded in response to the Supreme Coven." She regarded Holly sternly. "The Deveraux are very prominent within their ranks."

Holly raised her eyes, hopeful that help had come at last. She said, "How do we join up?"

Anne-Louise shrugged. "Your family has always been a member coven since we were founded. We . . . we regret that we did not contact you sooner." She blanched. "Our resources have been stretched."

"We've been fighting for our lives," Holly told her simply. "And we haven't been entirely successful."

Anne-Louise nodded. "Our condolences on your losses." She crossed her arms and legs and added, "All of them, including the death of the familiar, Hecate."

Holly reddened. Then she lifted her chin and said, "Two of my covenates have been kidnapped by Michael Deveraux. I would give anything to get them back."

"We have standards. We have limits," Anne-Louise admonished. "We do not sacrifice coven members, including familiars."

Holly moved her hands. "I didn't know—"

"We have always had problems with you Cahors," Anne-Louise cut in. "You're unpredictable. You're ruthless."

"Until a year ago, I didn't even know I was a witch," Holly protested.

"Witch blood runs in your veins," Anne-Louise cut in, gesturing to her. "Most witches would have been unable to sacrifice a familiar. They would have felt the wrongness of it." She made a fist and placed it over her heart.

"Well, it was wrong of you guys to leave us alone to face Michael Deveraux," Holly said. "I have to go to the bathroom. And I'm dying of thirst."

"Amanda won't be back. Not until I unward your doorway," the woman said. "And you will sit there and listen—"

Holly glared at her. The woman raised her chin. For a few seconds they had a standoff. Then the woman sighed heavily.

"Very well. You aren't my prisoner."

Saying nothing, Holly slid off the bed and walked unsteadily to the door. Truth was, she was shocked that there was such a thing as a Mother Coven to whom she was supposed to answer. And shocked, too, that they had left her and the others to twist in the wind for so long without backup.

But do something they don't like, and they're here in a hot minute.

She went into the bathroom and did her thing, then padded back to her room. The woman was standing and gathering her things: a black shawl, an overnight bag, and a purse.

"You're leaving?" Holly asked. "Aren't you going to help us with Michael Deveraux?"

"Yes. I am," Anne-Louise said in a clipped voice. "I've taken a room at a hotel, and I need to marshal my own powers. Alone," she added pointedly. "I don't want him to realize I'm here. I want him to assume you're still on your own."

Holly wasn't sure what to think about that. She said, "But you're helping, right?"

The woman hesitated. "As much as we can," she replied.

Holly crossed her arms and looked hard at the other witch. "You're afraid of him."

"Any wise witch is."

Holly could practically read her thoughts.

"You didn't want to come here. You asked not to."

The woman inclined her head. "That's also true." She cleared her throat. "I'm going to check in and perform my ritual. I'll get in touch in about six hours."

"We have about a day," Holly pointed out. "He said I had until the full moon." *To save them?*

To die?

The woman exhaled and slung her bag over her shoulder. She began to walk to Holly's door. "I'll be in touch." She added, in a weak tone of voice, "It's the best I can do."

"Pardon me for saying it, but your best sucks," Holly flung at her.

The woman turned her back to Holly and walked out of the room. She murmured something and made a gesture with her hand.

Amanda raced into the room, ignoring the witch. Holly realized Anne-Louise had cloaked herself with invisibility.

"I hate you, Holly!" she shouted. "I hate you for killing Hecate! How could you do that?"

Holly didn't have time to be kind. "If it could have saved Eddie, would you have killed Hecate?"

Amanda's mouth dropped. Holly pressed her advantage.

"Michael Deveraux is planning to kill Silvana and Kialish. He'll come after us next. Don't you think Hecate's death is worth it?"

Speechless, Amanda simply stared at her. Holly felt sick to her soul, and mean, and unlovable.

But she also felt strong.

★ ★ ★

This bears watching, Michael Deveraux thought, as he spied on Holly with a scrying stone from deep within the chamber of spells in his house in Lower Queen Anne, a neighborhood of Seattle.

His imp capered about the room, chattering at the skulls placed on the altar, laughing with mad glee as he glanced into the scrying stone, then darting away, his attention seized by some other object in the room.

Michael had witnessed her sacrifice of the familiar, which he had found both startling and delightful. *I didn't realize she had it in her to do something like that. She's far more blackhearted than I thought.*

He had also heard and seen her side of the conversation with the witch from the Mother Coven; the witch's side of the meeting had been hidden from him. But he knew what that meddler wanted; she was telling Holly to toe the party line: *no deaths among the good guys. But waste all the bad guys you want.*

When Holly had pretty much told her to go to hell, he had silently applauded.

I wonder if I've underestimated her, he thought. *Maybe I can turn her to the darker side. In thrall to me . . . or to Jer, if he regains his sanity. Her union with the Deveraux Coven would assure my rise to power in the Supreme Coven.*

No sooner had he thought those words, than he smelled the stench that often presaged the arrival of

Laurent, Duc de Deveraux, and his ancestor.

Sure enough, as Michael knelt in humble obeisance, the moldering corpse that was his ancestor stepped off Charon's boat as it glided into being in the center of the room. Sulfur mixed with the gut-churning odor of decomposition, telling of the hellfires Laurent had left in order to make the voyage back among the living.

"Laurent, it's been so long since you have made yourself known to me," Michael said. "I have wonderful news. I have two captives, and it looks as though I'll be luring Holly of the Cahors to her death."

"You liar," Laurent said in medieval French. He backhanded Michael, sending him sprawling to the floor. "You are thinking of sparing her. *Cochon.* Don't think it. The entire House must be wiped away from this world and all worlds."

His cheek throbbed as if he'd been branded. Laurent advanced on him, menace in every step.

"You want the Black Fire again, don't you? You want to rule the Supreme Coven. Then you had better kill the witch or you will never be able to conjure it again."

Michael took that in. His heart pounding, he tried to summon his dignity—and his courage—as he got to his feet.

"Then I'll kill her," he said calmly.

★ ★ ★

Anne-Louise had been a practicing witch from the time she learned to speak. She had grown up in the Mother Coven, a ward of it. Her parents had been killed shortly after she was born, so the coven had been both Mother and Father to her.

In her hotel room she meditated, gathering her strength. The coven had sent her because wards were her magical specialty. Diplomacy was her mundane one. Although, one would not have guessed that, given her confrontation with Holly. She shuddered. Being near the younger witch had been an unpleasant experience. Drowning the familiar had tainted her. The evil coming off of her was terrible to feel.

Two tears slid slowly down her cheek. The first was for the familiar, Hecate. The second was for the witch Nicole, whose cat Hecate had been. Anne-Louise prayed to the Goddess that their fates would not be the same.

She took several cleansing breaths trying to regain her focus. She was tired from the long flight and the encounter with Holly. Additionally the ward she had set at the top of the stairs when she left the house had just about drained her. The deep breaths helped refocus her attention, and she resumed her meditations putting the Cahors witch from her mind. Cahors were always such trouble.

London, 1640

"Kill her," Luc Deveraux whispered as he watched the proceedings. He had been tracking Cassandra Cahors ever since he had arranged for her mother, Barbara, to be burned at the stake. Now finally Cassandra would die as well and by another fine witch-hunter's tradition.

Dunking.

Onlookers gathered at the water's edge while the witch-finders in charge of her case spread across London Bridge to watch her drown, and drown she would. The commonly held belief was that witches floated. So, a woman accused of witchcraft was often thrown into a small body of water to see if she floated. The only way to prove that one was innocent was to drown and die. Much good innocence did for one.

Of course the common superstitions were all wrong. Witches didn't float. Cassandra Cahors would drown and everyone would believe she had been innocent of witchcraft. Nothing could be further from the truth.

He smiled, savoring the irony.

Tied to the ducking stool, she struggled beneath the water, then was pulled up in case she wished to make a confession. She looked like a drowned cat, all huge eyes, her hair beneath her mob cap plastered to her head. She was wearing down; her breath was very labored, and he was overjoyed.

Cassandra was dying, and as she looked out at the crowd, all the fires of hell burned in her eyes.

"I curse you, all of you!" she shouted. "You shall all drown, every one of you! As I die, so shall you."

Luc waved his hand and whispered a few incantations. He changed the spell, twisting it back toward Cassandra. At last he smiled triumphantly. "No, Cassandra. But all who love your descendants shall. I curse your house for all time.

"The loved ones of Cahors shall die by drowning."

Michael and Laurent: Seattle, November

Laurent, the mighty duke of the House of Deveraux, watched his descendant Michael attempting to hide his fear as he got to his feet, and his entire being flooded with rage. *To see my house reduced to this: a modern-day playboy who tries to play the game as the Cahors did. . . .*

Laurent possessed a ferocity and passion that, quite literally, had taken him beyond the grave. Catherine of the Cahors, his rival in life, had not managed to make that transition, and she spun through the universe as ashes.

Jean was dead because of them. True dead.

I will not have this. I have found the living Cahors witch, and I will see her dead.

Thus far, he had only been able to appear to Michael and to touch only him. But as he stood livid and furious, he felt strength rushing through his being.

Energy crackled around and through him; his head snapped back, and it was as if lightning had jolted through him.

Michael's eyes widened, and the duke realized that something was happening to himself; he glanced down at his hands and watched the gray, rotten flesh drop from his bones and soft new skin appear. He touched his face; the same thing was happening there.

In large clumps, his old body fell away.

He was becoming a man again—vigorous, filled with life.

At last. At last!

"Whoa," Michael whispered, impressed. Michael's imp chittered and pointed, leaping about the room.

"Did I not tell you that I would come back to this plane a full man?" Laurent chided Michael, although his heart was overflowing with shock. He had not realized it would ever really happen.

He took a step forward, and another. His ancient clothing fell away, leaving him naked.

He said to his many-times-great-grandson, "Fetch me clothing."

Michael raced off to do as he was told, his imp bounding after him.

Then Laurent closed his eyes and raised his arm; he whispered, "Fantasme."

The great falcon took shape and weight as he landed on the arm of his lord and master. His bells tinkled; he screeched softly.

Laurent opened his eyes and looked fondly at the bird.

"Ma coeur," he said. "My heart. Come with me, my beauty, and we'll hunt as we once did."

The bird cawed in reply.

Michael returned with clothing for him—a black sweater, black trousers, boots—and Laurent savored the sensation of fresh, new attire on his new body. He realized he was hungry. But that hunger would have to wait.

He had a witch to kill.

He strode past Michael, who called, "Where are you going?"

"To do your work," he flung over his shoulder, not even breaking stride.

His strong thighs propelled him up the stairs. He hesitated, unsure of his bearings, when the falcon lifted from his arm and fluttered down a corridor. Within a minute Fantasme had shown Laurent the way to the front entrance of the Deveraux home.

He moved his wrist and the door opened. As he crossed the threshold, he was tempted to turn the entire house into a raging inferno, be done with Michael Deveraux once and for all. But he reminded himself that, after all, Michael was a strong warlock who knew his family's proud history and longed to restore the family honor.

He's not all bad, Laurent thought.

He's just not me.

The moon was nigh full as its beams glowed over him. Michael was right to set the meeting with Holly Cathers on the full moon, which was on the morrow. His power would be greater for killing her then.

But Laurent was not going to wait that long.

He snapped his fingers and shouted, *"Magnifique!"*

Clouds roiled and scudded over the yellow moon, and stars blinked and shuddered. An arc of flame shot across the sky, and upon it, the mighty hooves of Laurent's warhorse, Magnifique, took form. They were followed by his legs and then his body. Flames shot from his nostrils, his mane, and his tail, and he cantered down from the sky to the ground, stomped his left foot, and dipped his head to Laurent.

"By the Horned One, I have missed you," Laurent said fervently. Then he climbed on the back of the horse, sans saddle. Fantasme rode on his shoulder, and the trio galloped down the streets of Michael's town, Seattle.

The skies cracked open and rain poured down. Steam rose off Magnifique's heavily muscled body, and Laurent threw back his head and laughed. Then he put his heels to the horse and they picked up speed, until the warhorse's hooves made the street sizzle and melt.

Fantasme showed the way; the dark lord of the Deveraux rode for hours; and then . . .

. . . he stood before the house where the witch resided.

Without a moment's hesitation, he galloped up the walkway toward the porch.

He fully expected there to be wards, and he conjured as he rode, breaking each one as he did so. He was surprised when he had disabled them all, expecting more fight in the young woman, and with a wave of his hand, flung open the door. Magnifique trotted inside.

He smelled smoke and remembered the night Michael had attempted to conjure the Black Fire through the sacrifice of Marie-Claire, the lady of this house. How livid Laurent had been that night! Michael had disobeyed him, putting that lady in thrall to himself—that minor Cahors witch, that adversary—after Laurent had expressly forbidden it.

He had materialized here and cuffed Michael, and hated him for his duplicity.

But would I respect a man who did not push, take chances? When has obedience mattered to the Deveraux? I would rather he take the initiative and accomplish great things than allow fear of me to limit him.

He raced through the living room. The hot winds of anger rose with him; Magnifique's body sizzled and burned from the speed at which he ran. Laurent reveled in all the sensations, and he laughed in anticipation of what he was going to do to that little witch, either carry her off and kill her slowly, or allow Magnifique to trample her as she ran.

He started up the stairs and—

—was blocked.

A powerful ward shimmered between him and the top of the stairway. Roses shimmered in it, and lilies, suspended as if in crystal.

He lips curled back in utter hatred. He changed spells and created from his hands an enormous fireball, which he lobbed at the ward.

Nothing he did had any effect.

The Mother Coven has been here. This is one of their wards.

He urged Magnifique on; the horse reared, as frustrated as his master. His large hooves slammed at the barrier, the magical energy shocking them both. Magnifique reared again and again, coming down hard on the ward. It would not give. Fantasme struck at it with claws and beak, and still it remained intact and in place.

And then, standing inside the barrier, a woman's shape shimmered and blurred. She looked at him with eyes he knew, with a sneer he knew too well. . . .

She lives on. I had not known that.

That threw him . . . but he found his composure as he regarded the ghostly image of his dead daughter-in-law.

"Isabeau," he proclaimed, "get thee hence. I abjure you!"

Her image wobbled but did not fade. She was staring at him with the same degree of hatred he felt for her. Tearing her apart with his teeth would be too good for her.

"You murdered my heir," he said to her. "It's only just that I take the life of the Cahors descendant."

She made no reply, but a strange smile ghosted across her lips, then was gone.

She raised a hand and pointed toward the front door, contemptuously dismissing him.

Laurent clapped his hands three times . . .

. . . and he, Magnifique, and Fantasme were magically transported back to Michael's chamber of spells.

Michael looked startled, but the two young people who lay tied up on the floor were terrified. The girl began to scream; the young man closed his eyes and began to chant. Laurent felt his attempt to send him back into the ether as a mild tickle across his sternum.

He dismounted and slapped the horse on the hindquarters. Fantasme perched on his shoulder, then glided over the two prone figures, screeching in anticipation. The bird had been taught to love tidbits of human flesh.

"You couldn't get to her," Michael guessed.

Laurent nearly hit him again for embarrassing him in front of mere captives, but he put his hands on his hips. He said, "The Mother Coven is here. Did you know that?"

Michael exhaled with contempt. "Who cares? A bunch of withered old nuns who are ineffectual at best."

"Tomorrow, the witch dies," Laurent ordered him, trying another tack. He smiled evilly at the two on the floor. "So you might as well kill them now."

"She's a *voudon;* he's a shaman. I'll get more power tomorrow if I kill them on the full moon."

"Very well," Laurent said, conceding the point. Then he touched his stomach and said, "I want to eat."

Michael nodded. "I'll take you upstairs and make you a steak."

They went upstairs.

Jer: Avalon, November

It was a freezing cold day, and Jer was starving. Healing took a lot of energy. James had jumpstarted the process, but it was far from over. He was still horribly scarred.

Bundled in a pea coat, a blanket over his knees, he sat on a stone bench and looked out to sea. He wondered what Holly was doing; if she dreamed of him. He would be surprised if she didn't. He knew that in his dreams, he called out to her.

I have to try harder not to do that. I will be the death of her.

There was a soft pad of footsteps. Jer looked up to see one of the servants cautiously approaching with a silver tray. Silver covered dishes gleamed on its surface.

Jer signaled for her to come closer. She was afraid of him, whether because he was a powerful warlock or because he was so horrible-looking, he had no idea.

He said to her, "What do you want to know today?"

She was shy; she said, "How to find money."

"All right."

She handed him the tray. They had a deal going. She told him any news she heard, and in return, he taught her simple spells.

"What do you have for me?" he asked her.

"James is back," she said. "He's got a girl with him. A witch."

That caught his attention. His hair stood on end; his cheeks grew hot as he wondered, *Have they taken Holly?*

"What's her name?" he demanded.

She cocked her head. "I want to learn how to find money and how to make someone I hate lose her glasses."

On any other day, he might have laughed. But today he said, *"What is her name?"* He lifted a finger and pointed it at her, an ominous threat.

She backed up. "Nicole."

Holly's cousin. She used to date my brother.

This could not be good.

He nodded and said, "Okay. I'll teach you. But first . . ." He took the cover off one of the dishes and smiled appreciatively. Fish and chips. He loved them.

He picked up a fry and began to pop it in his mouth when a terrible smell hit his nose. He froze, staring down at the fry.

Green energy shimmered around it, and its manifest aspect was that of a shriveled piece of rotting garbage.

Poison, he realized. *From Eli . . . or James?*

The girl watched him; she was curious, but there was no sign about her that she knew she had brought him food designed to harm him, if not kill him.

He put it back down. He looked at her and said, "Get me something else. Something you've had some of."

Her eyes widened at the implication.

Without another word, she took the tray and hurried away, as if she was afraid he would blame her.

He stared out to sea.

Nicole's with James. Are they upping the stakes, trying to get Holly to come here, to Avalon?

"Don't do it," he said aloud. "Holly, don't."

TEN

STRAWBERRY MOON

☾

Catch them now as they run
Kill the moon with the sun
We will take what they won't give
Cahors die so Deveraux live

Try to fight the sun god's power
Call on Goddess every hour
Fight them, kill them, don't give in
House Deveraux must not win

Seattle, November

In her hotel off Pioneer Square, Anne-Louise snapped wide awake. She lay still for a moment, allowing her memories of the past day to flood back in. One of her wards was under assault. It was the one she had placed in Holly's home. She closed her eyes, feeling the ward, feeling the energy assaulting it. Who was it? It was a Deveraux. Michael? No. She gasped and reached for her cell phone.

London, September, 1666

Giselle Cahors paced before the altar in the great house that was home to the Mother Coven in London. She was skeptical of the High Priestess's decision to move the Temple from Paris to this place, and not shy to state her opinion on it.

"London is barely large enough to hide one coven, much less two," Giselle observed.

"What would you have us do, child? Abandon the city to the Supreme Coven?" the High Priestess of the Mother Coven asked, raising her brows.

Giselle stopped pacing and put her hand on the carved folds of the wooden wall panel as she touched the athame tucked in the girdle of her full, black skirts.

"No, Priestess. I would have us *destroy* the Supreme Coven, not try to dwell in its stated territory."

"And with its destruction, destroy your Deveraux enemies?" The High Priestess sat back in her curved-back chair and folded her arms over her chest. She looked so like a nun, in her white wimple and robes, that Giselle had to remind herself that they were of the same tradition. "Is your concern for the Mother Coven or for your own house?"

"For both," Giselle protested.

The woman cocked her head. "My child, if your loyalties are divided, then you are not to be trusted.

The strength of your purpose must outweigh the call of your blood. We shall fight the Supreme Coven in our own time on our own terms. When our power grows to surpass theirs, then we can rid the world of their evil."

Evil. The word flowed silkily off the older woman's tongue, and Giselle could not help but shiver. Standing there in the inner sanctum, she stared at the altar and the blood stains on the floor all around it. It was a fine line that divided the Mother Coven's evil from that of the Supreme Coven.

"Very well, *ma mère*," Giselle bit off. "I will be the coven's obedient daughter."

"There's a good girl," the High Priestess said patronizingly. She reached out her arms to receive a ritual embrace. "Now, leave us. We have much to do."

With a hot heart, Giselle embraced her, dipped her head, and left the room.

This may have been a mistake, she thought.

Realizing she could not battle the entire Deveraux family alone, she had joined the newly formed Mother Coven, which was made up of witches who claimed to practice "whiter" magic than those of the more powerful Supreme Coven. Over the last few months Giselle had been given reason to question that claim.

Still, the leadership of the Mother Coven said all

the proper things about the superiority of white magic and made all the appropriate gestures to Coventry at large. To hear them, it was *she* who was the problem, she who was the bloodthirsty one. It was her Cahors blood that was tainted and evil and to be reigned in.

For the thousandth time she wondered what her grandmother, Barbara, had been like, and if she, Giselle, would have a different view of magic had the older witch lived to influence her offspring.

Thanks to Luc Deveraux she would never know the answer. He had been responsible for her grandmother being burned at the stake and for her own mother's life of running and hiding before he had finally caught her and had Cassandra Cahors drowned. He thought he had finally succeeded in wiping them out and had risen through the ranks of the Supreme Coven based on that accomplishment.

He didn't know that one Cahors still eluded him.

He would, though, soon enough.

She had seen him in her scrying stones. He was near. For weeks she had read the signs. They all pointed to the next few days. If she was to finally kill Luc Deveraux, she might never have a better opportunity.

Despite what she promised the High Priestess, she did not intend to let this chance pass her by.

I've made a few close friends among the other covenates, she thought as she strode down the corridor and away from the inner sanctum. *They might aid me in the coming battle.*

Luc Deveraux was older than he looked. Some shred of vanity prodded him to maintain his appearance. The magic kept his body alive, and with a little effort he could look well when he chose. His family had grown even more powerful under his tutelage, and their alliance with the Supreme Coven had only brought them more power. Within a couple of generations they might even be leading it.

Only the House of Moore posed a threat. The warlocks of that family seemed to grow more powerful by the day. House Deveraux needed to be focused in order to outwit House Moore and claim the throne of the coven, the seat of power. House Deveraux could suffer no distractions, no barriers. He had systematically removed all that he could think of. All but one.

She thinks I don't know about her, he thought, *but I do. I have always known about her.*

The signs were right. He would wipe the last descendant of the Cahors from the earth.

He has called me.
He has challenged me.

Giselle was thrown. She had thought to have the

element of surprise in her armory. She had also thought to have one more moon before she challenged Luc Deveraux to battle.

But he had thrown down the gauntlet first.

Drawn by his magics, Giselle and her two sister witches found themselves in Pudding Lane.

He was there, waiting, and he was not alone. The two groups approached each other slowly, silently.

They were met on the street as though on a battle-field. Luc and Giselle locked eyes, warriors about to do battle.

Without warning Luc pulled a wicked dagger from beneath his cloak and threw it with deadly accuracy toward her head. She lifted a hand and the dagger stopped in midair. It slowly spun in a half-circle till it was facing its master. She sent it back with all the ferocity she could muster.

It was the signal the others had been waiting for. The battle was fierce, the opponents equally matched. Dark forms spun and twirled by the light of the moon, dancing to their own macabre tune with steps only those attuned to dark magics could accomplish.

Around Luc and Giselle the others slowly fell away. A warlock turned to melt into the night and a witch followed him. Another couple's struggles carried them into a nearby street. At last the two of them were alone.

Slowly they circled each other, searching for weaknesses. Both were tired, both were running out of strength.

"I shall kill you as I killed your mother and grandmother before you."

"And I swear by the Goddess that this Cahors will avenge all whom you have slain. You shall not kill another of my kin."

She was exhausted and shaking, but Giselle could feel the rage rising in her, filling her and giving her strength. Her hands began to shake with the power that coursed through her. At last she let it out in a single shout.

"Incendia!" Fireballs appeared in the air before her. She hurled them at the old man, one after another.

Luc batted them out of the sky as if they were children's playthings. Several landed at his feet, sputtering and dying in the dirt. Two plummeted into a nearby watering trough. One flew through a window into the home of the king's baker. The last one he sent back to her.

She threw her hand up and the ball of flame stopped in midair. It vibrated for a moment, humming as each applied more and more force to it. At last it exploded in a shower of sparks that rained down in the street between them.

"I've seen better tricks from charlatans, my dear child," he sneered.

"Poor Luc. Did you think that you had ended the House of Cahors then? You didn't take into account that she had a daughter."

"Ah, but I did," he riposted. "And you will certainly not escape me now."

Before she could respond, flames erupted from the window of the baker's house and shouts came from within. A woman screamed in anguish, and around the Coventry witches and the warlock, houses stirred to life with flickering candles as sleepy residents rushed to see the problem.

Giselle and Luc stared at each other for a long minute. At last he gave a mocking bow before wrapping himself in a cloak of darkness and vanishing.

As the first faces started peering out of doors, she realized that she had no time to be discreet. She picked up her skirts and ran down the street yelling, "Fire!"

People burst from their homes and ran toward the blaze upon hearing her shout. Not a single one of them gave her a second glance.

★ ★ ★

The fire moved like a living thing, terrible in its ferocity as it swallowed houses, shops, and churches alike without discretion. As if the destruction caused by the licking flames was not enough, houses were pulled down one after another, destroyed in an attempt to stop the fire's path. The fire just laughed and leaped across the ruins of people's homes and lives.

Ministers preached farewell sermons as the flames approached their churches. Thousands of people fled, many with only the clothes upon their backs. Still the relentless flame pressed on. Many claimed that it was the hand of God, that His face had been set against London because of its great wickedness.

For days the inferno blazed its way across London. When at last it seemed to die out at Temple Church, it was only gathering its strength for one last savage run. The smoke and debris clogged the air until it seemed the whole world was on fire.

In the end, the fire killed many people and destroyed thousands of buildings. When the last flame had died, Giselle stood in Pudding Lane, surveying the damage. She could scarcely believe that she had been standing in the exact same spot a few nights before.

Tears stung her eyes. So much carnage, so much death. Luc Deveraux had not come looking for her, and as she stood staring at the chaos they had caused, she vowed not to hunt for him. It was too dangerous.

There was a ship sailing in the morning for the New World. She and her daughter and infant sons would be on it. In the Americas she would start over. A new life with a new name. The old one reeked of death.

Gwen Cathers would be on that ship. Giselle Cahors had died in the fire.

Luc Deveraux tried in vain to still the trembling of his limbs as he stood before the Supreme Coven. Any warlock would be a fool not to fear the judgment of the coven under the circumstances.

The coven leader, Jonathan Moore, could not hide the smirk on his face as the coven delivered its proclamation.

"Luc Deveraux, you have willfully disobeyed the law of the coven by making your battle with the House of Cahors a public one and thereby endangering us all." It was significant that the coven did not care so much about the fire and the destruction it had caused except as it might lead to exposure.

"Already several have been arrested in connection with the conflagration. Two of them are warlocks, members of this coven who foolishly followed you. The other is your manservant. This reckless disregard for the safety of the coven cannot be overlooked. House

Deveraux shall hold no place in the leadership of this coven, and you must step down as the head of your house."

Luc was stunned. Death he expected and would have accepted, but he had not expected them to censure his entire family. He opened his mouth to protest. "My actions are mine alone. Do not punish House Deveraux for what I alone have done."

Moore was having none of it. "It is no secret that House Deveraux and House Cahors have feuded for many years. These public uses of magic will stop here and now. House Deveraux must regain the trust they once enjoyed in this coven."

So there is hope. Luc's agile mind began to consider strategies. He asked humbly, "How might we prove our loyalty?"

There were a few murmurs that were quickly silenced. Moore narrowed his eyes and thought for a few moments.

"House Deveraux must cease all displays of public magic immediately and forever. Also, your coven may eventually redeem itself by bringing the secret of the Black Fire to the Supreme Coven."

Luc felt sick in the deepest recesses of his twisted soul. The secret of the Black Fire was lost. House Deveraux could never redeem itself without it.

Philippe: On the Spanish border, November

They were going to burn José Luís's body.

They had waited the requisite three days to see if he would rise. But the warlock was truly dead.

Philippe wondered for a brief moment if it had been the death José Luís envisioned. He shook his head slowly, grief stricken.

Mon vieux, he thought fondly, *the battles we fought!*

Pray for me in Paradise that I will fight one to save Nicole, and win that one.

Several feet away the others huddled. Armand sat on the ground, too injured to stand. Seated beside him, Pablo was shaking with exhaustion. Philippe felt his throat constrict as he gazed upon José Luís's little brother, who looked so much like him. Alonzo crouched, eyes alert and probing the darkness, a cross in one hand and a crystal in the other.

He looked back down at the shell that had housed his friend and mentor. José Luís was dead, Nicole taken, and the battle against darkness had been well and truly joined.

He passed his hand over José Luís's face, blessing him. "We lost this time, old friend. But I swear to you, we shall prevail in the end."

He bowed his head briefly—half-praying, half-meditating. When he was finished he stood up slowly, his face set. He felt old and tired, but he knew what he had to do.

The others stared at him, seeking guidance, direction. He would give it to them. "We are going to find Nicole and battle this evil before it spreads farther."

"Where do we go?" Alonzo asked.

"Pablo?"

Pablo raised his head and in a weak voice answered, "London. They're taking her to London."

Philippe nodded. "Then that is where we shall go."

The others nodded agreement as he locked eyes with each of them in turn. Armand held his eyes the longest, and Philippe winced at the pain reflected there. Armand was more seriously injured than he had let on.

Philippe knelt beside him and placed a hand on his chest. Slowly he exhaled as his heart sped up to match the rapid beating of Armand's. Blinding pain surged through his body as his nervous system linked with Armand's. His body was trying to help heal the other warlock.

Suddenly the pain lessened dramatically, and Philippe opened his eyes to see that Alonzo was beside him, also working to heal Armand.

At last the most dangerous injuries were healed and the three broke contact. Philippe rocked backward on his heels.

From the torch stand, he plucked the flaming torch and touched the wood beneath José Luís's body. "As soon as he is ashes, we leave."

Seattle, November

The full moon was drowned by the heavy rains that fell from the sky in large, gulping cascades. Pioneer Square was awash; the twinkling funk of Hill Street was inundated; the bay was gorged and overflowing. It was not a fit night for anything, much less a battle. But it was the full moon, and witches were at their strongest.

Warlocks, too, but there was nothing to be done about that. Holly had called the Circle together at Dan's house. It was a beautiful, hand-built cabin in the woods, almost too small for the gathering that had assembled: Holly, Amanda, Tommy, Tante Cecile, Kari, Dan himself, and Uncle Richard.

"We have to get him out of town," Holly said to the group. "He won't be safe here no matter the outcome. He hasn't been safe here for months." She was speaking of her uncle, who was seated beside Dan's cast-iron stove in a state of shock. Back at the Anderson home, she and Amanda had revealed the truth about everything that was going on: the reality of Coventry, the fact that they were witches, that Michael

Deveraux, who had been his wife's lover, had also probably murdered her.

"But . . . but she had a heart attack," Richard had protested weakly. He looked so upset, Holly was afraid he himself might have a heart attack. So they performed for him, she and Amanda, conjuring the equivalent of witch parlor tricks. They conjured fire and wind, and they levitated objects in the room.

Then Holly produced a scrying stone, and asked him to look into it. He saw Michael Deveraux in robes, bowing before what looked very much like a Black Magic altar covered with skulls and black candles and a large book bound in black leather. The stone also showed Silvana and Kialish bound with ropes, their faces wan and bloodless. They might have been dead, except that at one point Silvana's eyes opened, and she stared in the direction of the stone's field of view, as if she knew it was focused on her.

Perhaps it was then that he began to believe. At any rate, he agreed to accompany them to Dan's, sitting in stunned, exhausted silence. Holly and Amanda had agreed not to tell him about the imp they had pulled from him and drowned, nor the fact that they had tied him up in case he tried to kill the two of them. He didn't remember any of it, and they thought it best to leave him ignorant of those recent dark days.

At Holly's request, Dan was going to purify each one of them for the coming rescue attempt. Each would go into his sweat lodge alone, hopefully to have a vision. Then he would speak to her of the shadow she had seen, and help her to use it to fortify herself in the coming battle.

At her request, everyone had dressed in the colors of the ancient House of Cahors: silver and black. She and Amanda were dressed in black sweaters and black leather pants, with silver hoops in their ears and silver chain necklaces from which dangled amethysts and silver. Dried herbs had been braided into their hair. Tante Cecile had plaited their hair, Amanda's into French braids and Holly's into corn rows.

Kari was swathed in a silver-and-black shawl over a black silk blouse and black jeans. Tante Cecile had on a form-fitting black dress embroidered with gold and silver leaves at the hem. Tommy wore black slacks and a T-shirt. He had borrowed a silver bracelet from Amanda, and he wore it awkwardly.

We used to be so many more, Holly thought. Then she reminded herself, *We defeated them on Beltane, on the 600th anniversary of the massacre of Deveraux Castle. We can defeat them again.*

"We have to assume Michael may launch an attack on us at any moment," Holly reminded the others.

"He has spies and scrying stones too. So I should go first. I'm point."

The others agreed.

Holly took off her clothes in Dan's bedroom, then wrapped herself in a large beach towel and followed him into the sweat lodge. Dressed in a T-shirt and buckskins, he stoked the alder smoke for her, sitting on his haunches while she inhaled the scent and began to sweat. The combination of smoke and heat made her dizzy; she allowed the sensations to take her over, and then the spirits showed her Pandion, the lady hawk, perched on her arm. Isabeau was riding Delicate, her mare, and the sun was shining gloriously down on her dark, unruly hair. She was galloping; her skirts of velvet were flying behind her, and Jean was shouting, "Slow down, wench! You'll break your neck!"

She cast a glance over her shoulder at her husband, laughing at him because he was having trouble keeping up with her. They were in the forests outside Deveraux Castle, and she was in love with him.

Never mind politics and magic spells, she was young and beautiful, and he was likewise young and very handsome . . . and the day was filled with joy. Above Jean's head the Deveraux falcon circled and soared in wild abandon, as exuberant as the witch and warlock. Then he screeched and dove into the thick underbrush. A battle ensued.

"He's caught something," Isabeau said delightedly, pulling on the reins. Delicate slowed.

"As have you," Jean replied, trotting up beside her. "My heart."

And then she was Isabeau, cradled beneath Jean as her kinsmen burned his castle to the ground; as his own kinsman Laurent conjured the Black Fire and sent it sweeping through the bailey. She could hear Jean screaming; could hear herself begging him to forgive her.

Through centuries they had searched for one another, locked in love and heat . . .

. . . and then a lady hawk flew above a misty island, dropping down, down, to land on the arm of a man who was so horribly, terribly scarred:

Jer.

Then overhead something wheeled, but it was not a bird; it was an Orca, a black-and-white whale, and it floated and swam. *I'm underwater. I'm drowning.*

She was beneath the waters of the bay, and as she turned to the right, she saw Eddie in the grip of the hideous monster that had killed him; and to the left, the rest of her coven, caught in the grip of its minions, each struggling to make it to the surface, their eyes bulging, unable to move as the creatures held them down.

They will drown.

She was spinning as if someone had tossed her out of a window headfirst; the vertigo made her sick and she crouched forward to vomit . . .

. . . and that was when she opened her eyes and came back to herself. She was back in the sweat lodge.

To one side of the sweat lodge was a shower; Holly rinsed first in warm water, and then in cool, allowing her mind to sharpen. Tommy went in next.

While she was there, Holly dressed and emerged from Dan's bedroom, facing her coven sisters, Kari and Amanda. Dan, who had finished helping Tommy get started, came out of the sweat lodge and regarded her soberly. It was he who spoke first.

"You want to go alone."

She replied, "I don't want to. I have to."

"No," Tante Cecile insisted, rising. "He has my daughter. I'm going with you."

"We all go together, or we all die here and now." Amanda spoke, pale and shaking with the force of her convictions. "He hurts us only when we are weakened by the absence of one or more. If we all stay together, we can all protect each other. It is our only chance of survival."

"I can't protect you," Holly protested, weakening under the onslaught.

"Who made you queen of the universe?" Kari asked sharply. "No one's asking you to protect us. If anything, I'm here to make sure you don't screw up again and hurt anyone else I care for."

Her reference to Jer and the fire that had nearly killed him was like a slap in the face. Holly took it, though she felt a growing animosity toward Kari that she knew she would not always be able to quell.

Anne-Louise watched from a safe distance as the members of the coven one by one entered the sweat lodge and took part in the ritual. Things were about to get very ugly. She could feel it with every fiber of her being. The only question was: What should she do to stop it?

Part Three
Waning

☾

"And when Lithia has passed and the year is waning there will be a great
pall that settles upon the earth. Some will be given in marriage whom should not and
others will wield a power unforeseen and uncontrolled. Then the earth will tremble
and the skies will rain fire."

—Lammas the Elder

ELEVEN

BLESSING MOON

☾

Fill us now, Lord, with your might
Help us now to end this fight
And we will defile the head
Of the Cahors Coven dead

Evil about, evil without
Don't let it turn you inside out
But as we turn from their sin
We find it naught to the evil within

Michael Deveraux: Seattle, November

In the day, Michael mused as he held his athame up to the candlelight and admired the very, very sharp blade, *a Deveraux warlock facing battle would have received last words through runners or carrier pigeons. Deveraux warlocks even conjured with smoke signals, back in the Wild West. Phones are much more magical, carrying our disembodied voices across space, and yet they seem far more mundane. The romance is lost, somehow.*

No matter that I have magically enhanced the connection, because of the rain.

November in Seattle was not a kind month. It was harsh and wild and angry—warlock weather. Samhain—Halloween in the parlance of humanity—had passed by without the proper obeisance from him. For the first time in his memory, he had not run his life by the esbats and sabbats of his tradition. Instead he had focused his energies on the Cahors and on regaining leadership of the Supreme Coven—an internally driven calendar based on ambition . . . and revenge.

"Why *not* try for a hostage exchange?" Eli asked. He was still in England keeping an eye on the Moores for his father. And watching his brother.

Jer, my errant son.

And if truth be known, my pride and joy. . . .

"She won't sacrifice herself to save two people who aren't even related to her," Michael said. "She's a Cahors, after all. The best I can hope for is that her coven will put the screw to her to make a rescue attempt."

"It's gotta happen, Dad," Eli murmured, lowering his voice. "You've got to kill her. Sir William's got them all totally freaked out. Some of them want to take you out."

Because of the attack on the ferry, Michael knew. *There's some flaw in me,* he thought. *I could've been more subtle. So why wasn't I? Deveraux rush in where angels fear to tread.*

"Don't sweat it," he drawled. "I'm this close to conjuring the Black Fire again. Then past history won't matter a damn."

Just past ancestry.

Everyone knows the Deveraux should rule the Supreme Coven.

He changed the subject. "What's the situation with Jeraud?"

"He's still on Avalon. James has done a lot to make him feel better, but he sure looks gross."

"So you've seen him."

"From afar. I'm at the headquarters in London."

You've probably been trying to kill him from afar too, Michael thought. *If you manage it, you'll be sorry. Jer's the one who has made the connection with Jean and has the power to show for it. Not you.*

There's some reason we were able to conjure the Black Fire last Beltane, and we have to find out why we haven't been able to repeat our success. And I don't think the answer lies with you, Elias.

"So, are you, like, challenging her to a duel? Inviting her over for hot wings and a Mariners game?"

"I thought I'd let her come to me," Michael told his son. He added, "I'll be in touch."

"But—"

"Good-bye, Eli."

He hung up and put the cell phone on the altar.

Michael was one of the premier architects of Seattle, and as such, quite a wealthy man. He had a lot of disposable income—not an unusual situation for a warlock of his stature—and much of it he had spent on a beautiful yacht, which he had christened *Fantasme*. When he took friends out, they were piloted around the bay by Michael's captain, a man named Hermes. But when he was alone, Hermes revealed his true aspect: He was a fiend, a servant of Hell, and had been in the employ of the Deveraux family for sixty years. He had taken quite a liking to Michael's little imp, and the two were having a grand time above deck, navigating the yacht through the black waters of Elliott Bay.

There had been discussion about closing the bay down entirely, then shutting it down to pleasure craft, then the entire matter had been dropped simply because the Coast Guard did not possess enough manpower. Michael had worked many obscuring spells and chants of forgetting, and the majority of the population had decided that there had not been monsters in Elliott Bay, but a renegade Orca and a school of sharks.

Also, as with any warlock of means, Michael's yacht was equipped with a fine altar to the Horned

God. His personal grimoire was placed next to the skull of Marc Deveraux, his father and a worthy warlock in his own right, and the cell phone next to that. A statue of the God loomed over the bowls and candles of the Rite, it being very similar to the one back in the chamber of spells in his home.

He bowed low, making obeisance, naked beneath his red and green robe, which was covered with signs and sigils. They matched the ritual scars with which he had decorated his body as a testament to his art. The blood from the original cuts had fed his blade well.

Now he turned to his two distraught prisoners. Propped up back-to-back on the floor, they were both bound and gagged without ceremony, he cut off one of the braids of the female and nicked the left cheek of the male. His athame sucked greedily at the young man's blood, and he shivered with delight, feeling the power as it built up in the blade.

He flicked his finger at the Hand of Glory on the altar—the shriveled hand of a dead man, from which five black candles glowed. Then he loosened his robe and drew a long line down the center of his chest with the tip of his athame. The blood poured freely.

"I call upon the God," he said in a loud voice. "I summon the powers at my disposal to aid me in battle. I seek revenge against the House of Cahors, and I call upon my imps and my demons, my fiends and my kinsmen, to aid me. I call this three, three, three; I call this seven, seven, seven, seven, seven, seven, seven. Abracadabra."

He could feel the power rushing through him and around him. Memories of long dead kinsmen filled his mind, and he began to chant in an ancient tongue that not even he knew.

Swirls of green, blue, and red materialized along the wooden floor, rolling like carpets of mist and smoke, gathering momentum and tumbling upon one another. From the porthole window, the flash of lightning illuminated the terrified faces of Kialish and Silvana as the mist crept around them, slithering up their bodies and dancing along their skin. Thunder rumbled, joining the bass roar of the yacht as Hermes opened her up.

Then the sound changed. There was a deeper bass line, which gradually took on a rhythm—*ka-thun, ka-thun*—as the mist grew thicker, folding in upon itself repeatedly until it reached Michael's knees and came up to the chests of his victims.

"I call upon my forebears," he yelled above the noise.

Ka-thun, ka-thun . . . the distant pounding of horse hooves. Inside the mist, prone skeletons began to form and take shape, solidify, and rise to their feet. Shields appeared, strapped to their arms, and swords. Others materialized with rifles and six-shooters. Then more— the modern Deveraux—took shape as moldering corpses, machine guns and Uzi's slung over their arms.

Ka-thun, ka-thun . . . Michael smiled as the mist completely filled the cabin, engulfing the two young people. Eagerly he crossed to the ladderway, his athame in his fist, and climbed up to the deck.

He beheld a glorious sight: the phantom hundreds of his kinsmen, riding on horseback down from the sky, driving up from the depths in sleek cars, cantering and racing to join the battle.

At the head of the skyriders, his standard bearer to his left, Laurent, Duc de Deveraux, rode astride Magnifique. His armor gleamed in the mist; Magnifique was armored as well and wearing the skirt of a warhorse, decorated in green and red.

The dead wailed with glee and a thirst for vengeance; as the Deveraux assembled, horned demons and imps popped into being. Red-skinned, long-knuckled fiends joined them, and the hellhounds bayed and globbered for witch blood.

Then came the falcons—hundreds of them.

All ready to gouge out eyes and pluck hearts from chests.

The duke rode down onto the deck, and Michael lifted his chin as he saluted him. In response, the duke took off his helmet and held out his hand.

"Well done," he said to Michael. "Perhaps you'll pull this off."

Surrounded by her coven, Holly stood underneath a black umbrella at the water's edge and watched hell fill Elliott Bay. Kari was staring through binoculars and muttering, "No freaking way."

Beside her, Tante Cecile murmured a spell and Dan slowly shook his head, looking stricken.

Amanda left Tommy's side, sidled up to Holly, and put her hand in hers, joining the two parts of the lily that they two bore as brands.

"Where's the Coast Guard?" she asked.

"Hell with the Coast Guard," Kari said. "Where's the National Guard?"

Dan shook his head in a perverse sort of admiration. "He was cleverer this time. He's cloaked everything. I doubt anyone else can see it. This show is for us and us alone."

"Then he knows we're here." Kari's voice was shrill.

"He wouldn't be much of a warlock if he didn't," Dan ventured.

"Then why not attack?" Amanda asked, licking her lips. "Why stay out there?"

Holly closed her eyes. "Because he's surrounded by water."

And he wants my covenates to drown.

Leaving me alone to face him.

I can't let that happen.

She watched as the dead army of the Deveraux continued to mass; they were thousands against six.

Holly closed her eyes.

Isabeau, I call upon thee, she pleaded. *I can't fight them like this. I need your help. I am a Cahors. Bring on my kinsmen and their allies and their servants in the arts. Save us . . . and I will give you whatever sacrifice you wish.*

Something churned inside her; she felt herself falling and tumbling; she was going into a very cold, very dark place. All around her, stars danced; there was no ground, there were no walls. She was in space. The stars stretched and glowed.

She was outside time.

Vivid colors swirled around her, blacklight and silverflash; purple, scarlet, cyan. Bursts of light danced and flamed out; stars fell by the hundreds.

She heard screams and wailing; she heard a single woman's voice whispering, "My daughter, my daughter, my daughter . . ."

Mom? she wondered excitedly.

But it was not her mother who called.

It was Isabeau's.

In a cloud of glowing rainbows, a woman shimmered into being. She was tall and imperious, wearing a double-horned headdress and clutching a bouquet of lilies to her breast. Her gown was black and silver, bunched up in yards of fabric around her feet. Her mouth was bound shut; she was a corpse being prepared for burial. Her eyes opened and she looked straight at Holly.

Are you worthy? she asked without speaking.

Holly swallowed hard. She raised her chin.

I have to be, she replied.

Are you worthy to carry the mantle? the ghost demanded. *They have all failed me, all. No one has ever taken Isabeau's place; brought our house back to its former glory . . . Are you the one? Should I bother sparing you?*

"Yes," Holly said.

She opened her eyes.

In the driving rain, Holly was surrounded by phantom warriors from other times and places, some carrying the standard of the lily, others waving swords. There were Cahors with crossbows and Cahors with spears.

When they saw that Holly had opened her eyes,

they raised their halberds and their maces and their swords and shouted, "Holly, Queen!"

Holly gasped and looked around for the others. They had moved about one hundred yards farther down the beach. She was alone in the tornado that was her army.

A lady hawk fluttered down and hovered beside her; Holly raised her arm and the bird landed with ease. Then a young man materialized in front of Holly. He was wearing a tunic and leggings, and he led a massive warhorse by its reins. He knelt down and offered her the stirrup.

Holly understood; she put her foot in the stirrup, and somehow she had the wherewithal to hoist herself up and onto a boxy saddle made of bone and metal. The bird stayed firmly perched on her arm.

Armor magically covered her; the world narrowed through the slits of a helmet.

"Vive la Reine!" the army chorused, hoisting their weapons into the air. *Long live the Queen!*

Holly took a deep breath. *I have absolutely no idea what I'm doing.*

The other members of her circle scrambled toward her; she hurtled them away with a bolt of magic from her fingertips. Falling end over end, they managed to get to sitting positions, looking quite astonished.

"You'll drown," she said, but she knew they couldn't hear her because of the wild war cries and cheers around her.

"*Alors, mes amis!*" Holly cried, though she had never spoken French in her life. "We shall kill the Deveraux once and for all!"

"*Deveraux, la-bas!*"

Her squire handed her a lance, just like in the movies about tournaments. Banners fluttered from the shaft; the head glowed a poisonous green. Though it was massively heavy, she hefted it into the air as if she would spear the rainclouds themselves.

Thunder rumbled; lightning flashed. The dead of the Deveraux wailed and shrieked. Their falcons were more numerous than raindrops.

"Holly!" Amanda shouted. "Holly, take us with you!"

Holly paid her no mind. *Live,* she thought to her cousin.

Then she put her heels to the flanks of her warhorse and cantered toward the water. Cheering wildly, her soldiers followed her.

As soon as the horse's hooves hit the water, it galloped on top of the waves, sending out flumes of water as it hastened to the battle. Steam issued from its nostrils; tiny flames danced along its back and mane.

Holly's entire being tingled and jittered as if she had been plugged into a huge machine. She felt the connection between her and each member of her army . . . and she saw Isabeau on one side of her, and Catherine, Isabeau's mother, on the other side, although she knew they were invisible and what she was seeing was a sympathetic vibration in her mind.

Like volleys of cannon, she and her troops flew across the water. The Deveraux falcons began to dive-bomb at them; Holly raised her lance and conjured a spell. Fireballs issued from her lance, taking out dozens of the birds; then another fireball followed, and more.

Others of her army did the same. Corpses of dead falcons plummeted into the water.

From the center of the Deveraux storm—the yacht—horsemen and soldiers took a cue from their leader and raced toward Holly and her hordes. The sound was deafening; Holly could hear nothing; and yet, she could hear the thundering of her heartbeat—

—and someone else's—

Her lance crossed the lance of a Deveraux whose face was a skull. Though she had never jousted before, she pushed hard against her enemy's lance, and to her astonishment, he dropped it. In her left hand a sword materialized. She raised herself in the saddle, leaned over the horse, and stabbed the skeleton in the rib cage.

It exploded.

She blinked, but had no time to process what she'd seen as more Deveraux converged on her. She swung her sword and aimed her lance as if she had been born to battle; the lady hawk fluttered at her ear, chirruping as if she were giving Holly directions. It felt to Holly as if she were actually guiding her arms and legs; she had no idea how to fight like this, and yet she was doing a superb job.

Down the Deveraux fell, and down, exploding into nothingness; her army was astonishing in its daring and skill. Whooping and yodeling with pure wanton battle lust, her warriors attacked with fearless abandon.

Holly fought just as well as they; and when she realized that she was actually making headway toward the yacht, she was so amazed, that she was nearly taken out by a hideous creature dressed in skins and a helmet topped with a human skull.

But it was there! She could see the navigation tower and the thing inside it, an imp larger than the one she had drowned seated on its head. The yacht was flying through the water as if Michael were retreating, but Holly knew that would be too good to be true.

"*Allons-y!*" she shouted, gesturing to half a dozen of her ghostly companions. She pointed with the tip of her sword at the yacht. "We'll board her!"

"Non, non," a voice sounded in her head. "Below decks."

Her horse galloped at an angle, its hooves working underwater. A line of portholes gleamed with magical energy at Holly's eye level.

She knew deep in her soul that Silvana and Kialish were inside.

"Attack!" she shouted.

All around her, her fighters launched themselves at the line of portholes, smashing them with sheer bodily mass—startling, for they were phantoms—and Holly's horse flew into the gash. It was pitch black inside.

The vessel immediately listed and began taking on water.

Holly leaped off her horse into the icy bay, slogging waist-deep, shouting, "Silvana! Kialish!"

Her right knee hit something; she reached down and grabbed a head of hair. There were two of them.

They're tied together.

She felt down farther and found ropes, gathered her hands around them, and began to struggle back toward the gash.

The yacht was going down.

"Horse!" she shouted.

Her horse chuffed at her, and she dragged the nearly dead weight toward it.

How long have they been under? Goddess, protect them, keep them alive. . . .

Then, with strength she knew she did not possess, she hoisted them up out of the water.

In the moonlight she saw the faces of Silvana and Kialish, slack and empty, and she feared the worst. But there was no use worrying about that know.

With her sword she cut them free, trying to position them so that they would be able to stay on the horse. But they were too limp.

"Help here!" she bellowed.

Two phantoms rode up. One was a skeleton; the other was dressed in the soggy clothing of a Jamestown Puritan. Each took one of the stricken comrades without comment, laying them in front of them over their saddles.

Holly slapped the horses' flanks and said, "Back to shore."

The horsemen complied.

Then all at once, the yacht went down.

Coughing and vomiting water, Kialish regained consciousness. He was staring straight at the yacht when it sank beneath the surface. That was shock enough; what was worse was that Laurent, the ghostly leader of the Deveraux, dove in after it astride a huge black horse.

In his right hand he carried a wicked-looking sword. In his left, a magic wand.

The water he dove into glowed blood red.

Kialish closed his eyes. *He's after Holly.*

By the change in the troops around him, he knew he was right. Those who still had faces looked stricken; skull jaws dropped open. Heads tilted back. There was screaming such as Kialish had never heard before. Fear boiled around him.

The Deveraux saw their panic and redoubled their fight . . . and Holly's army began to falter.

All this Kialish saw with a strange, lockstep clarity. He knew what was happening almost before it occurred.

He also knew that Laurent was going to kill Holly . . . unless something could be done.

Something can be done, said a voice inside his head. *You can do it.*

Though he was being carried along at breakneck speed, a woman's figure shimmered in front of him. She was holding a mirror, and she gestured for Kialish to look into it.

He saw Holly drowning Hecate. He knew why she had done it.

She needs to give something more to the water, the figure said. *Something of value.*

The figure faded, then vanished, her mirror with her. The red glow where he had last seen Holly bloomed and spread like blood on the water.

Kialish thought of Eddie, and his heart ached.

You will see him again. I swear it.

He thought of all the things he had planned to do with his life.

You will do other things, on another plane.

And then quickly as he could, so that he couldn't be saved, Kialish heaved himself into the water.

It was black, and filled with energy and things that moved; as something dove into the water above him— his rescuer, perhaps—something else grabbed on to his ankles and began to pull him down into the water, too far down to breathe, ever again, even though within seconds, his lungs were screaming for air . . .

. . . and then in a shimmering sphere, he saw Eddie, his arms outstretched; he stretched out his own, or thought he did; his mind was fuzzy and he was starting to die. But there was Eddie. . . . Yes . . .

. . . and he loved him, and he would be with him. Yes.

And the Goddess took what had been offered her, upon the water.

TWELVE

HARVEST MOON

We savor all the death we cause
Tear the bodies with teeth and claws
Drink the blood and eat the flesh
Quickly now while they're still fresh

Cahors now have too much power
We glory in our unholy hour
Twisting, turning they will writhe
As we harvest them with scythes

Holly: Seattle, November

The coven went to Dan's, though the shaman had taken Uncle Richard to San Francisco to keep him from harm.

Now, facing her covenates, Holly couldn't meet their eyes. She had done something horrible. She could feel it in the weight of the stares on her. Still, in her very core, defiance stirred. She had done what she had to, what was necessary to save them, all of them.

Except Kialish.

She couldn't stop the tears that burned the back of her eyes. Kialish was her failing, though she knew he had chosen to sacrifice himself to save her. Had she not needed saving, had she been more powerful, then he would still be alive.

She closed her eyes, remembering what it had felt like when he died. There had been one intense moment of pain followed by a surge of power unlike everything she had ever felt before. Even the water seemed to push back from her as though in awe of the energy crackling through her veins.

Holly has lost it, Tommy thought as he stared at her. She swayed slightly, and he wondered what she was seeing, what she was feeling. Beside him Amanda sat and he could feel her anger and her fear. Holly was beyond them now.

He would never forget the terrible things he had seen the night before, watching, helpless, from the shore. *It shouldn't be this way. It isn't right.*

He stared around at the others and knew they were thinking the same. He knew that Kari was thinking of leaving the group; she had all but said it. He would go if he could, but he was bound. Still, his loyalty was to Amanda, not Holly. If Amanda chose to follow Holly then he would too.

* * *

Anne-Louise could still feel her heart pounding in her chest. It seemed as though it had not slowed since the battle's end. The news she had to deliver to the Cathers witches from Mother Coven had done nothing to soothe her nerves. The thought of breaking that news to Holly just made her heart pound harder.

Holly was unlike anything she had ever seen. The young witch's power was tremendous, greater than she even guessed. In time she would learn how to use and harness her power. She would be nearly unstoppable then. Now, though, she was still too wild, too untrained. She wasted much of her strength, and she had no idea of the unplumbed depths within her.

Anne-Louise could not help but wonder what Holly would be like had she also been raised in the coven. She would be more skilled, stronger, certainly more controlled. *And maybe none of this mess with the Deveraux would have happened.*

She shook her head. That wasn't true. As long as there were Deveraux and Cahors alive there would be a blood feud. It was a shame, such a waste of time and magic. The rift between the two families was too great, though, for even her to mend. Some things couldn't be fixed with words. Some truce's couldn't last and sometimes peace could not be forged.

She smiled wryly. Not that anyone was even trying to do those things. No, the feud between the two families was permitted, perhaps even secretly encouraged by both the Supreme Coven and the Mother Coven. The power of House Deveraux and House Cahors was too fearsome, and the only way either coven had truly found to control it was to keep it focused elsewhere. As long as Deveraux and Cahors were fighting each other neither could take over one of the covens . . . or the world.

She cleared her head of such thoughts; it would not do to have them read by others. She took a deep breath. Time to face Holly and her coven.

She passed through the wards without needing to break them. It was a trick that, so far as she knew, she alone in Coventry could do. It was a lost art, mentioned only once in one of the ancient texts. It had taken her fifteen years to learn to do it. It came in handy, though, whenever she wanted to arrive unannounced.

Holly and company stared up at her in shock as she lifted her veil of invisibility and appeared in their midst. She surveyed the ragtag group, noting their injuries, both the physical ones and the mental ones.

She wished that she was bringing them comfort. Unfortunately it was quite the opposite.

Nicole: London, November

Nicole had to admit that it felt good to bathe. She had been given some privacy, or at least she thought she had. As she disrobed she couldn't put from her mind the thought that someone might be spying on her. She had fought the urge to dive into the bathtub, clothes and all. Instead she had forced herself to undress slowly.

She was enough of a performer to make a good show of it, even if her hands were shaking. Now, as she lay in the steaming bath, she scrubbed away all the dirt with a loofa and vanilla-scented soap. Rose petals floated in the water.

She felt more like a virgin about to be sacrificed than a bride. She shivered despite the warmth of the water. As she sunk lower in the water, she thought of how she had nearly drowned in the last bathtub she had been in. She vaguely remembered a foolish vow never to take another bath and only to shower. But that was before the dirt.

Her mind drifted back over the past twenty-four hours. Sir William had been furious when James had presented her. She hadn't needed any special powers to sense that. Not half as furious as Amanda and Holly would be if they knew. She couldn't help but smirk weakly at the thought.

Would they think that she had lost her mind, or worse, her heart? Amanda would probably think the worst. After all, in the good old days hadn't Nicole gone out with Eli, attracted to his darkness?

What would Amanda and Holly think when she didn't come home? Would they look for her? Were they okay? Amanda had tried to tell her something, something about a ferry, but she had had no time to listen. *She said that Eddie was dead.* Nicole had not known him well enough to mourn him, but still she shuddered. Things could not be good back home. They probably needed her, and now she couldn't go to them.

I'm not flaking on you, Amanda. I just can't get out of this one.

She closed her eyes and fought the urge to explode into giddy hysteria. Amanda didn't know her anymore. She barely knew herself.

No, in the old days she would probably have been attracted to James. She freely admitted it. That was back when she confused dark with strong, before she had felt the power of the Light. Before Philippe had held her while she cried.

Her heart ached at the thought of him. She knew he would be coming for her, but he didn't know when. Her job was to stay alive until he did, no matter the cost, no matter that she had to marry the devil to survive.

The Cathers/Anderson Coven: Seattle, November

"What do you want?" Amanda asked, breaking the silence.

In the shaman's house, Anne-Louise stared unblinkingly from one to another. "You, all of you. Holly has been summoned to meet with the Mother Coven in Paris, and everyone is to come along."

"Why should we?" Holly asked.

"Because we can help you." Anne-Louise continued to hold the room a moment longer. Finally she stepped backward, and everyone started talking all at once.

She waited patiently for several minutes. At last everything had been discussed and Holly rose to her feet. Anne-Louise stepped back to the group.

"We will go, but not all of us. Tante Cecile and Dan are taking Uncle Richard to San Francisco. There they will protect him and also look out for an old friend. Amanda, Kari, Tommy, Silvana, and I will go with you."

Anne-Louise nodded understanding. She disguised her relief. The discussion had gone better than she had dreamed.

★ ★ ★

The private jet was standing by at the airport, and Holly could not help but gawk. They were ushered inside by Anne-Louise and were soon seated in the softest of leather chairs.

"Drinks and food are in the galley," Anne-Louise informed them, pointing. "Help yourselves."

Tommy, eager to be of help, jumped to his feet and raced off. He was back in moments with sodas for all and little bags of nuts.

"Ever think of becoming a flight attendant?" Kari quipped.

"Travel, meet interesting people, gain unique life experience? Sorry, I think I've had my share of those," he answered good-naturedly.

Holly gazed at Tommy. The young man was not a warlock, not truly, but he tried so hard. When he handed Amanda her soda, his smile brightened and he brushed her hand.

Holly stared in turn at Amanda, wondering if her cousin knew how Tommy felt about her. If she did, she didn't let on. *Either break his heart or give him some bit of hope,* Holly thought.

As though she had heard her, Amanda turned and gave her a tight smile. Holly smiled weakly in return before settling back in her chair. It was going to be a long flight.

Gwen: Atlantic Ocean, 1666

The storms had raged for days all around the ship. Everywhere, people were sick and dying. Giselle, now Gwen, had gathered her children—she had three—and left London. The Mother Coven was furious with her, and she had no use for them.

Now she chanted spells of protection over her twin boys, Isaiah and David, and Marianne, her daughter. The four of them were still healthy, Goddess be praised. The people needed fresh air, needed to get away from each other. At last one of the crew informed her that the rain had stopped.

She gathered up her children and went up on deck. Around them the ocean churned, but a pale stream of sunlight cut through some of the clouds. She breathed in deeply and urged the children to do the same.

Marianne scampered away from her across the deck. Gwen did not stop her. The child needed the exercise, needed the freedom.

When Marianne walked over to the side of the ship and peered over into the water, though, Gwen felt her heart move into her throat.

"Come away!" she shouted.

But it was too late.

A massive wave swept over the side of the boat and sucked the child with it back into the sea.

Gwen lurched forward, screaming. The captain had seen, and he stopped her, pushing his body between her and the side of the boat.

Two crewmen ran over to the side and peered into the dark waters. Slowly they straightened, shaking their heads grimly.

"I am sorry, madam. She is gone," the captain told her in a gruff voice. His eyes, though, gleamed with sympathy.

She screamed and tried to throw herself after her daughter. Maybe she could still save her. She could at least join her.

"Madam! Think of your other children!"

The words brought her to her senses. She turned, sobbing, and ran back to her two small boys. They looked up at her with fear shining in their eyes. She crushed them to her and wept.

By the time the forests of the new land came into view, she had resigned herself to the death of Marianne. Her heart was broken, but she was a Cahors, and broken hearts had little to do with what must be done.

Now we are three, we "Cathers." I have no daughter to carry on the family line, but the boys have at least some magic. Mayhaps 'tis just as well. Perhaps it is a sign from the Goddess that House Cahors is truly dead . . . and that the magic should die with me.

Gwen of the Cahors looked down at her boys and felt only love for them. She wanted them to grow up knowing only love. And peace. No, she wouldn't teach them the magics. She wouldn't tell them of the Goddess and their sworn enemies, the Deveraux.

It would all die with her. The cycle would be broken.

Her daughter was the last sacrifice. "No one else shall die because of our family," she swore to herself.

She gathered the children in her arms and took them to the rail.

"Look, my children. We are coming to a new world. A new place. It is called Jamestown."

A cloud passed over her joy.

Jamestown had been named for King James, the monarch who had so detested witches.

No matter, she reminded herself. *All that is over.*

The Mother Coven: Paris, November

"It was nothing short of miraculous," Anne-Louise told the High Priestess as they sat together in the

Moon Temple. The circular room glowed with luminous paintings and holograms of the moon, graced with golden-yellow candlelight and verdant pools of fragrant water. Ancient mosaics to Artemis decorated the floors; the walls were covered with murals and sacred writings to the Moon Lady, who was the Goddess in all her aspects.

Acolytes moved soundlessly, tending the flames of the many candles and braziers, heaping lilies and roses at the feet of the statues of the Goddess in her many incarnations: Hecate, Astarte, Mary of Nazareth, Kwan Yen, and others.

The Moon Temple was the most sacred space of the Mother Coven.

They were sipping covenate wine; Anne-Louise had requested and been granted rites of purification upon her return. She still wasn't certain if she had been cleansed of Holly's taint. She didn't feel as whole and strong as she had upon her arrival in Seattle.

"Miraculous is an odd word for a witch to use," the High Priestess observed. She was an older woman, still very beautiful, with long red hair tumbling around her shoulders. She was dressed in the white robes of her office, with a moon tattooed onto her forehead. Anne-Louise also wore white flowing robes.

"The Deveraux disappeared," Anne-Louise continued, waving her hand so violently that she almost spilled her wine. "The entire army simply disappeared." She leaned forward. "The Mother Coven *must* protect her . . . no matter what she does."

The High Priestess looked thoughtful. "But she's a Cahors . . . blood will out. That boy who died . . ."

Anne-Louise shook her head. "Would you rather that she joined the Supreme Coven? They highly prize ambition and power. What if they facilitated a truce between her and the Deveraux?"

The High Priestess scoffed. "Sir William Moore would never allow that. It would pose too great a threat to his leadership."

"Sir William has many enemies," Anne-Louise said reasonably. "Our only hope is to stand by Holly, let her know that we are her friends."

The High Priestess regarded the other woman for a full minute. Then she said simply, "So mote it be."

They raised their glasses of wine in salute, took a sip of wine, and smashed them on the tiled floor.

Paris, November

The room was humbling; even Holly felt the power of it and dropped her eyes reverently. The Moon Temple was beautiful and filled with peace and light. The High Priestess had greeted them briefly and then withdrawn. Anne-Louise stood to the side.

There were half a dozen other women spread throughout the room, all staring at the new arrivals. One of them moved toward Holly. Her silver hair cascaded to her knees.

It was the woman from her dream. She moved with the same grace in the flesh that she had in Holly's vision. She strode forward and very solemnly kissed Holly on each cheek.

"Who are you?"

The woman gave her a ghostly smile. "My name is Sasha. I am Jer and Eli's mother."

Beside her Kari gasped. Sasha turned toward her. "And you, my friend, know me as Circle Lady."

Holly was shocked to see Kari throw her arms around Sasha and begin to sob.

THIRTEEN

DARK MOON

☾

Darkness covers all we do
Fills our souls through and through
Death and evil lurk in our wake
What Deveraux want Deveraux take

Goddess guide us through the night
Fill us with your will and might
Grant us will to carry on
And chase away the fateful dawn

The Cathers/Anderson Coven: Paris, November

In her white temple robes, Holly walked by the light of
the waning moon in the robe garden, savoring the
tranquility of the Moon Temple compound. It was
amazing to Holly that such a vast complex could be
located within the city limits of noisy, busy Paris. But
the place was very peaceful, warded against the hub-
bub and the chaos, and part of her wished she could
become an acolyte and live here for the rest of her life.

They have no idea what it's like beyond these walls, she thought. *They've forgotten. Or is it that we're more jacked into reality, aware of the evil in the world because we're fighting Michael Deveraux?*

Someone was following her; she sensed a vibration in the air, the soft pad of footfalls on the smooth-stoned path that meandered like a snake through the garden. She closed her eyes and murmured a spell of Seeing, then relaxed as she saw that it was her cousin.

She walked slowly so that Amanda could catch up. Amanda's white robe was a little long on her, and she had gathered up the extra fabric in her fists; she looked like a little girl playing dress-up. Holly smiled wistfully for younger days, happier days.

"They sent me to find you," Amanda said by way of greeting. "They're getting ready for a strengthening ritual for us."

Holly took that in. *They know we're leaving.* They had only been there one day and one night, but she knew too that they could spend no more time recuperating from their battle with Michael and the long flight to Paris.

"Tommy and Silvana are already there," Amanda went on, then added, smirking, "Kari says she's not going to participate, and she wants the High Priestess to get someone to drive her to the airport."

"*So* not a team player," Holly observed, then realized that she was hardly one to talk.

A beautiful-sounding gong rang three times. Amanda turned to Holly, who said, "Let's do it."

They walked the serpentine path together, turning along a hedgerow to face the entrance to the Moon Temple. The entrance was a fat arch of stone, the building topped with a dome shaped like half a grapefruit. Beautiful plane trees, commonplace in France, flanked the entrance; before each tree stood an oversized white marble statue of the Goddess in one of her aspects, as within the temple: Astarte, Diana, Jezebel, Mary of Nazareth, and Mother Teresa.

Amanda stopped abruptly. She put a hand on Holly's forearm and whispered, "Look, Holly."

The statue of the Goddess as Hecate was crying. Tears streamed in rivulets down the stone face.

Holly swallowed. Moved, she slowly knelt on both knees and bowed her head. Amanda watched, her features soft, and Holly said silently, *My cousin thinks I'm begging your forgiveness, Goddess Hecate. But I only did what you wanted, and I refuse to believe that the familiar's death is my sole responsibility.*

The statue's tears stopped.

Holly had no idea what that signified, only that some sort of response was implied.

"Oh, Holly," Amanda whispered as she stared at the statue. She took Holly's hand and helped her to her feet. "Holly, I . . . I'm sorry I've been so mean."

Holly was sorry too, but not in the way Amanda meant. She was sorry that Amanda's apology meant nothing to her, except that it was proof that Amanda wasn't strong enough to lead the coven.

I've changed so much, she thought. *After I sacrificed Hecate, I got tougher. And with Kialish's death . . . my heart has hardened.*

Well, so be it. If this is what I have to become in order to keep my coven alive and save Jer, then that's fine with me.

They entered the temple together, moving through the foyer to stand beneath the rotunda, which was made of alabaster and allowed the moonlight to shine through. Then they walked through another smaller arched entrance to the temple proper, and they both drew back.

There were probably two hundred women dressed in white robes lounging throughout the temple room. They reclined gracefully on white satin pillows or rested beside the pools, which were floating with roses and lilies. There were no chairs, no rows of seats—the seating was very casual, haphazard, and fluid.

They look like cats, Holly thought.

A large stone table had been erected in the center

of the temple under a second dome not visible from the exterior of the building. The High Priestess stood behind it, opening her arms in welcome to Holly and Amanda. She wore a headdress of silver topped by a crescent moon sparkling with diamonds. Moons had been tattooed with henna on the backs of her hands and on her cheeks.

"Welcome, Cahors. We salute you."

Amanda glanced sideways at Holly and whispered, "Why is she using the older version of our name?"

Because in Coventry it's who we are, Holly wanted to tell her. *We're not Cathers and Anderson.*

We are the House of Cahors. For all we know, you, Nicole, and I may be all that is left of the line.

"Welcome, Cahors," the white-robed women chorused throughout the temple.

"Come forward, Circle," the High Priestess intoned.

Silvana and Tommy rose from beside a statue of the Goddess and came toward the High Priestess. Like everyone else, they wore white temple robes, but Silvana's dark hair hung free over her shoulders. Tommy looked awkward in the white robes among all the women, but he gave them a brave smile.

At her urging, Holly and Amanda came forward as well.

The High Priestess kept her arms held out and pivoted in a circle as she continued.

"We are here, sisters, to strengthen and protect this, our daughter coven, as they prepare to leave these walls."

Holly couldn't help her reaction of disdain, lifting her chin and frowning as she thought resentfully, *We are not a daughter coven. We're a separate, independent entity. We haven't agreed to let them boss us around.*

But the other women in the room murmured, "Blessed be," signifying their approval of the High Priestess's sentiment.

She motioned for Holly and the others to kneel. They complied, Holly bracing herself for whatever came next.

A lovely young girl with delicate Asian features glided to the High Priestess's side. She was carrying an alabaster bowl; the scent of lavender wafted from it.

"We anoint you with oil," the High Priestess intoned. She dipped her fingertips in the bowl and lifted them up. Lavender-scented oil dripped from them.

She and the girl moved first to Silvana.

"Goddess, protect this girl's eyes." Silvana blinked, and the High Priestess placed her fingertips on Silvana's closed eyelids.

"Goddess, protect her lips."

She touched oil to Silvana's mouth.

"Protect her heart."

It went on. Holly's mind began to wander.

I don't belong here. The Mother Coven is out of touch, out of date. I need to work with a stronger group; people who aren't afraid to use the hard magics to fight the Deveraux and the Supreme Coven.

She pictured harder, tougher women, not so soft and anxious.

Amazons, Holly thought. Her mental image expanded to include herself, astride her ghostly warhorse, commanding the ghost army back on Elliott Bay.

I need to find more women—correction, more people— who have the guts to fight like that.

". . . and aid them on their quest to save the third Lady of the Lily from the clutches of our enemies. . . ."

Lady of the Lily?

"Blessed be," the women lifted up in heartfelt prayer.

"So as they go from this place to save their sister witch, Nicole Anderson—"

"No."

Holly stood, forcing the girl holding the alabaster bowl to step anxiously back. Some of the oil spilled out of the bowl onto her sleeve.

There was a collective gasp.

"Holly?" Amanda murmured.

"We will go to Nicole," Holly assured her cousin, "but first—"

"No," Amanda cut in, rising to her feet. She said to the High Priestess, "You know what she wants to do."

The priestess nodded, then said to Holly, "Nicole is of your blood. Your duty is to her."

"I have no duty!" Holly thundered.

Then it was as if someone had placed a kind of shimmering, projected field in front of her. From her perspective, everything and everyone in the temple was bathed in blue light. She looked down at her hands and saw that they, too, were covered in blue.

"Isabeau," Amanda said, staring open-mouthed at Holly.

Holly's mouth opened, but it was not her voice that spoke.

"*Alors,* we came to you for courage, for strength. But you are so weak! This one and this one alone will save the Mother Coven and prevent the Supreme Coven from enslaving all humanity! And she will do it with the aid of our enemy's own son, Jeraud Deveraux!"

The High Priestess moved directly in front of Holly, as if shielding everyone else in the temple room from her.

She's afraid of us, Holly thought with glee.

Amanda spoke next.

"Isabeau," she said, her voice faint but steady. "I know why you want to go to him. Your husband can take him over, just like you're doing with Holly."

"Silence!" Isabeau launched into a barrage of what Holly, standing aside as Isabeau took her over, assumed to be medieval French.

Then Isabeau forced Holly to press both her hands together. A glowing sphere of blue energy formed between her hands. It tingled and sizzled, teasing the skin on her palms. She slowly rolled and shaped it into a ball, and it burst into flame.

The women in the temple reacted instantly. Some cried out; some ducked. All except for one who stood slightly off to the side, her face obscured by her hooded robe. Holly's eyes were drawn to her. There was something about her. . . .

Her attention moved back to the others as they scurried out of the way. Holly was exhilarated by their expressions of fear and of respect. Even the High Priestess withdrew, putting at least fifteen feet between them.

I'm with you, Lady Isabeau, she silently told her ancestress.

Ma brave, Isabeau replied. *What a fine witch you are!*

"Don't push us!" Holly cried, savoring the moment. And with a rush of pure joy, she raised her hand menacingly over her head, aiming the fireball at the nearest statue of the Goddess—

—*Hecate again!*—

—and as with the statue in the garden, the statue in the temple began to weep.

Holly was instantly jerked out of her reverie.

What am I doing?

Do it, do it, Isabeau urged her. But her dominion of Holly had ebbed.

Flamed-cheeked, Holly lowered her arm. The fireball vanished.

Then Isabeau was gone. Holly felt the connection break as surely as if someone had disconnected from a phone call.

Aghast at what she had said and done, she rushed into Amanda's arms and murmured, "I'm sorry, Manda. I'm sorry." She burst into tears.

"It's all right," Amanda murmured. But the fear that lingered in her tone gave the lie to her words.

Her face against her cousin's shoulder, Holly said, "We'll go to Nicole. We'll save her."

Sir William, James, and Nicole:
The Supreme Coven headquarters, November

Sir William looked on with great pleasure—and wistful envy—as Nicole Anderson, bewitched into mute obedience, placed her hand in his son's. Sir William himself bound them together with herb-soaked rope and cut their palms to mingle their blood.

He'll bed her, take her power, lure the remaining Cathers witches here, and then I'll have all three of them burned alive on Yule.

The news had just come in: Holly Cathers and what was left of her coven had just snuck into London for the express purpose of saving Nicole.

He was amused by how cautiously they skulked about; José Luís's coven had done the same. Didn't they realize that London was the home base of the Supreme Coven? That nothing that went on here escaped notice?

Nothing. *Surely James knows I'm aware of his many plots and schemes to depose me,* he thought as he beamed at his son the bridegroom. *Michael Deveraux must realize that as well.*

The Deveraux are such wonderful loose cannons. One never knows which way they'll aim . . . and once their fuses are lit, whom they will hit.

It makes life interesting. And when one has lived as long as I have, that's a rare and precious gift—precious enough to keep dangerous foes alive when they should be rotting in the garden with their eyes gouged out.

Before him, the little bride, swathed in black from

head to toe, swayed slightly and blinked her eyes. In those eyes he read her horror and dismay to find herself utterly powerless to stop the marriage. She could not speak, could not refuse to marry James.

Happy to rub salt in that wound, Sir William lifted up the cup into which their blood had been dripping and toasted them, saying, "It's done. You're married."

Then, almost in the same breath, he turned to a very young and very ambitious warlock named Ian, whose real ambition was to become a producer-director in Hollywood, and said, "Search for Holly Cathers and her followers and take them down. If you can't contain her, destroy her on the spot."

Michael, Eli, and Laurent: Seattle, November

The moon had waned and waxed, and now it was full again. The Anderson family mansion was deserted. Polite inquiries had yielded the information that Richard Anderson had relocated, at least temporarily, although neither the phone company drone, the utility minion, or the travel agent Richard usually used could tell Michael where they had gone.

None of his scrying arcana in the house could tell him either.

No matter. I'll find him soon enough . . . if I need him.

He stood in the backyard of the fine mansion with Laurent and Eli, who was newly back from London with the news that James had married Nicole.

Eli had gotten the distinct vibe that it might be time to step well away from all the intrigues in London and reassess his position. He had not been able to kill Jer— *yet*—and he had figured out that before he managed it he'd better have a significant peace offering to give his father, or he might end up dead as well.

"There it is," Michael said, pointing to a rosebush in the backyard. Roses did not normally bloom in November, at least not in Seattle, and yet the bush was bursting with color, despite the fact that moonlight usually bled red to gray.

Then Fantasme the spirit-falcon appeared in the sky and flew down to join the party. Michael smiled in greeting, and Eli nodded. Laurent sighed with pleasure and held out his arm. In his living days, Fantasme had been his boon companion on many a day of hunting.

Then Michael got down to business. He took a deep breath and found his center, then spread his arms wide and spoke to the earth.

"I bid thee, rise, and become one of mine," he commanded.

Thunder rumbled in the distance and it began to rain.

Michael did not move, but repeated the incantation a second time. "I bid thee, rise, and become one of mine."

The rain came down harder.

"We should have brought umbrellas," Eli muttered. Laurent silenced him with a harsh glare. But that was all he did. The great lord of the Deveraux had already started adjusting to the realities of modern life . . . including mouthy young many-times-great-grandchildren.

Lightning flashed again.

"I bid thee, rise, and become one of mine."

The rosebush shook and an ungodly howl of fury echoed from beneath the ground.

As the three looked on, the muddy earth from which the rosebush grew began to shift.

A yowl issued from the mud, followed by a low, menacing hiss.

"I command thee, live," Michael said, flinging wide his arms.

A single paw shot up from the mud. Then the mud heaved; in the pouring, hard rain, the dead familiar,

Hecate, wobbled onto her four legs and blinked her golden eyes.

"I have given you back your life," Michael said to her, "which was taken from you by the witch Holly Cathers. Will you serve me now?"

Hecate opened her mouth.

"I freed you from death," he reminded her. "Will you serve me now?"

She shuddered.

"I will," she said.

That done, Michael wheeled around in a circle, inundated by the storm. The winds howled and screamed; lightning flashed and crackled.

"Who else?" he demanded.

The rain poured down and clouds raced across the moon. "Who enters my service? Who joins my coven?"

"I will," came a chorus.

Hecate jumped into his arms. He petted her fondly as, all around him, forms took shape: dead men, dead women, gnomes and spirits, disfigured demons, and imps bearing the scars of torture.

Michael understood. They were who had come up against the Cahors before and been cut down, often savagely. The Cahors had never shown their enemies any mercy—a fact which Isabeau had conveniently ignored, in her so-called "plan" to spare Jean from burning to death. The need for revenge was so great in these who had answered his summons that it had kept them earthbound—a kind of living, if one stretched the definition.

"We'll find her together," he promised them. "And we will make her and her coven pay for everything every Cahors has ever done to any of us."

"For everything," the bled, gray dead chorused.

Michael smiled at them and at Laurent, who looked on approvingly and said, "*Bien.* Well done."

Michael replied, "I promised her I would kill her by midsummer. And I will."

Jer: Avalon, December

On Avalon, Jer paced his cell, listening to his informant as she told him, "The Cathers/Anderson Coven is said to be in London. Sir William and James are searching for them everywhere."

I must not send my spirit out to her, or they might track her, Jer thought, stricken by the news. *I told her to stay well away from me . . .*

. . . but she isn't in London searching for me. She's looking for her cousin.

He was both glad and disappointed. But that was not important.

She must live.

Isabeau and Jean: Beyond Time and Space

Isabeau ran to Jean, her arms outstretched, but the hatred on his face made her legs give way. She crumpled to the ground before him, murmuring, "Forgive me, my darling. I tried to save you. I did not want you to die by my hand."

"Yet obviously you swore to another to do so," he riposted, "and so we chase one another through time, locked in hatred."

"*Non, non.* In love," she insisted. "In love, *mon* Jean."

The look on her face entrapped him, charmed him, hexed him. She was his Isabeau; she was his love. . . .

"*Ma vie, ma femme!*" Jean cried. *My life, my woman.*

He fell onto his knees before her, gathered her up in his arms, and kissed her.

Jer kissed Holly in his dreams. . . .

In her dreams, Holly kissed him back.
"Jer," she whispered, sleeping. "I will find you."

Aaron Corbet isn't a bad kid—he's just a little different.

On the eve of his eighteenth birthday, Aaron is dreaming of a darkly violent and landscape. He can hear the sounds of weapons clanging, the screams of the stricken, and another sound that he cannot quite decipher. But as he gazes upward to the sky, he suddenly understands. It is the sound of great wings beating the air unmercifully as hundreds of armored warriors descend on the battlefield.

The flapping of angels' wings.

Orphaned since birth, Aaron is suddenly discovering newfound—and sometimes supernatural—talents. But not until he is approached by two men does he learn the truth about his destiny—and his own role as a liason between angels, mortals, and Powers both good and evil—some of whom are bent on his own destruction....

the
fallen

a new series by Thomas E. Sniegoski

Book One available March 2003

From Simon Pulse

Published by Simon & Schuster

BASED ON THE HIT TV SERIES

Charmed™

A magical incantation invokes in the three Halliwell sisters powers they've never dreamed of. As the Charmed Ones, they are witches charged with protecting innocents.

But when Prue is killed at the hands of the Source, Piper and Phoebe believe the Power of Three to be broken.

That is, until their half-sister, Paige Matthews, arrives at the Manor, with a few tricks—and a few questions—of her own....

Look for a new title every other month! Original novels based on the hit television series created by Constance M. Burge.

Available from Simon & Schuster

WICKED

LEGACY

Enter a new world of power ... and fear

Holly Cathers and her twin cousins, Amanda and Nicole, are college students who are also the last descendants of the medieval witches of the House of Cahors. Forming a new coven, they ally themselves with the forces of light and set out to end the vendetta that has ruled—and ruined—their family's history for centuries.

Holly has traveled to England to save her imprisoned soulmate, Jer, who is a member of the House of Deveraux—and the Cathers' worst enemy. But following dangerously on her heels is Michael, Jer's father and head of the Deveraux coven, who is looking to derive ultimate power from a witch consort.

Holly learns that her uncle and her mother's best friend are in grave danger, and that she must enter the Nightmare Dreamtime and battle demons and other forces of darkness in order to save them. But can Holly successfully fight these horrors, *and* safely return home?

by Nancy Holder and Debbie Viguié

AVAILABLE SUMMER 2003
FROM SIMON PULSE

FLOOD OF MAGIC

Holly Cathers and her twin cousins have just graduated from high school, and they're moving on toward their first semester of college. But no matter where they go, they will never be entirely free of their past. The three are descendants of a powerful coven of witches—in constant danger from a rival clan.

Holly learns from a vision that Jer is still alive. As leader of the coven, she resolves to rescue him despite the fact that he is a member of the Deveraux clan and therefore her enemy. But her efforts are thwarted when her aunt reveals the nature of an ancient curse visited upon all Cathers witches. It becomes clear to Holly that the death of her parents was no accident, and a similar plague is sure to fall on anyone she grows close to. As her power strengthens, can Holly escape her destiny? And if her destiny includes Jer, does she want to?

Don't miss the first title in this new series!
WICKED: WITCH

⋀⋀⋀ **SIMON PULSE**
Simon & Schuster, New York
*Cover illustration copyright © 2003
by Kamil Vojnar*
Cover design by Russell Gordon
www.SimonSays.com
0103